MISPLACED DANGER

A Fatal Prescription

Marla K. Morris

SPECIAL THANKS

Special thanks to Erika Lee, Monica Grey-Childs, Beulah Robinson, Joyce Sheppard and Kathy Brinston who are some of the first among my loyal fans. Shout outs to Toski, Candace and Khai Morris, and Maria for reviewing my rough and raw manuscript. Thanks to my son, Patrick Morris, who clued me in about The Falcon. I appreciate each one of you. I hope you all enjoy reading this fictional work as much as I did creating it.

PROLOGUE

About five years ago, there was a viral YouTube post demonstrating how the head start in life generated by and for privileged individuals exacerbates racial inequality.* Head starts in the race for a hundred dollar bill were given to contestants who didn't come from broken and impoverished homes. The same advance in the competition was granted to those who had the benefit of a private education. Conversely, those who were given a "dead start" came from homes that were particularly lacking. They were left behind because they lacked a father figure in the home, adequate nutrition, and guaranteed access to education. Those "left behind" contestants were overwhelmingly people of color. The key point was that being given clear advantages made this race called life much easier for some, yet markedly difficult for others.

This narrative showcases how the capital city residents are interconnected like those in a much smaller rural town. The desires of the rich and powerful are achieved at the expense of the livelihood of the poor and powerless. It explores how failures in the home and community compound into thwarting the personal success of two very different men. One man managed to continually progress with his distinct privilege while another man struggled but somehow attained a modicum of success without it.

*Life of Privilege Explained in a $100 Race
Peter D. Linkyear. (2017, October 14). Social Inequalities
Explained in a $100 Race. [Video] YouTube retrieved from
https://m.youtube.com/watch?v=4K5fbQ1-zps

Chapter 1

How Did We Get Here?

As Teddy Robinson got older, he gained an appreciation for his atypical upbringing. He lived in a nugget of affluence, called Eastgate, that was juxtaposed to the poverty-stricken Near East Side of Columbus. His family home was on the proverbial right side of the tracks. Their cottage-style home was nestled on the other side of the South Greenway train viaduct. Although he came from a broken home, his mother was blessed with a job as a registered nurse. Her earnings afforded them a comfortable lifestyle envied by some of his classmates who were barely surviving on the other side of the tracks living in tenements, apartments and lean-to shacks. Perhaps his comfortability was what kept him tethered to his childhood home.

"Teddy! Did you get my cigarettes? I'm tired of smoking these Kools. They're not my brand. You know that," Thelma admonished her son who had failed to replenish her supply of Balmoral cigarettes. Balmorals were imported and Teddy could only buy them at a special smoke shop in the nearby ritzy suburb of Bexley called The Tobacco Leaf.

"No, Mom. I haven't had time. When I leave work, I'm exhausted and I just want to get home. I'm trying to work all the overtime I can in case our department gets eliminated by the upcoming reduction in force. I'll be sure to stop tomorrow," replied Teddy from the living room as he rolled his eyes. Luckily, his mother couldn't see his insolence because she was parked at the kitchen table gazing out of the bay window, her constant perch. She had to be the nosiest neighbor in a 100-yard radius. When Teddy was in middle school, she became disabled. No longer being able to work, she had turned herself into a housebound recluse. She relied on him to bring whatever she needed from outside into their quaint cottage-style home. There was an unspoken role reversal. Instead of a mama bird bringing food to her chickadees, Teddy was the offspring delivering sustenance to his mother.

"You've been saying that for three days now. Did you spend my cigarette money? Are you trying to force me to quit?" Thelma asked.

"Forgive me Ma if I just don't have time to ensure *your* habit is amply supplied. When are you going to start getting out more? Being a little more active? Aren't you supposed to be getting at least fifteen minutes of fresh air a day? Dosing your Vitamin D from the sunshine? Isn't that what your therapist suggested?" he asked.

"Well, the same quack tried to send me to hypnosis to stop smoking. Some good that did me," she said snubbing out the flame on her second-rate Kool cigarette.

"Mom, you know as well as I do that you are capable of doing so much more than holding down that neighborhood spy chair. Your health and outlook will improve once you get active and get those endorphins moving through your body. You always feel better when you exercise with those Richard Simmons Sweatin' to the Oldies VHS tapes. You don't have to run a marathon, but you can try walking around the neighborhood every now and then."

"Oh Teddy, my days of being physically fit are long gone. Did I tell you I used to run track? I was fast as lightning. Fast and cute. At fifteen, I was the Pumpkin Queen too. I got the medals and a crown to prove it. I was the "it" girl back in my heyday. Then I met your no count Daddy and . . .," Thelma began her diatribe about her ex-husband, Teddy's father.

"Yeah, yeah, yeah. I've heard it a million times before Mom. He single-handedly ruined your life and I indirectly ruined your figure," Teddy said sarcastically.

"Well, he did," Thelma said and began to cry.

"Mom, don't you think you're being a little dramatic about a man you've been divorced from for over twenty years now?"

"No," she sniffled and dabbed at her eyes. "Those were the best and worst seven years of my life. I was so happy being a wife and mother. Then like that," she snapped her fingers, "he left us. No argument, no warning, no rhyme nor reason, just poof! He disappeared. It hurt my heart so. He stole my youth and yours too. You were only five, but you've had to grow up so much faster with it being just the two of us."

"That's so heavy. I'm still not going to get your cigarettes, but nice try."

"Teddy, sometimes I think you like making light of my situation."

"No, Mom. You just don't like when I don't agree with you. Your current situation is you're out of *your* brand of cigarettes. It's not an urgent matter. There's no need to call a Code Red. You'll live. You've been divorced from The Person Who Shall Not Be Named for over two decades. While tragic, I am sure it hurt like hell back then, but by now hasn't your heart healed just a teensy-weensy bit?" he smiled at his mother while holding his thumb and forefinger slightly apart.

"Get on outta my face! You always think you know everything. Wait 'til your kids torture you like you do me." Thelma realized her antics were not going to move her headstrong son. She lit another subpar cigarette and resumed her spying on the neighbors.

"Did I get any calls?"

"Let me remind you that I'm not your secretary, but no," she replied and exhaled a long plume of smoke.

"Are you sure?"

"Why wouldn't I be sure? Why would I lie?"

"Uh, because you don't like any of my friends."

"What friends? Those fast tail girls who don't bother to speak to me with some decency. Them hussies and heifers you call 'friends'. Nope. None of 'em called."

"Mom, you never have given any of them a chance. Anyway, if they do call, then I'll be upstairs in my room," Teddy patted his mother on the shoulder as he went upstairs to the attic-bedroom he considered his true domain in the house. He prided himself on not being the typical bachelor living in his mother's basement. In the story and a half structure, his triangular shaped bedroom was his little corner of heaven on Earth. He nicknamed his hallowed space the Nifty Nest. He fancied himself the personification of Stan Lee's Falcon, the first Black comic book superhero. He regularly fed his alter ego falling headfirst into the vivid pages of his extensive collection of Marvel comic books. He had an affinity for all things *Dungeons and Dragons*, *Space Odyssey*, and of course the Ohio State Buckeyes. There were colorful posters of all his favorite things plastered on his sloped bedroom walls. A mainstay was his moving three-dimensional model of the Solar System he'd entered and won at a 1974 citywide Science Fair in high school. Being a fan of volcanoes, he had a framed 1500-piece jigsaw puzzle outlining their structure. His room was accessible only by climbing fourteen steep stairs. Thankfully, his mother had not ascended those treacherous steps in years giving him ample privacy.

* * *

As a sophomore in high school, Teddy accidentally became a social butterfly. As an only child, he was somewhat sheltered. Finally, he had been allowed to attend Ivette Hamilton's sixteenth birthday party. She lived in a cul-de-sac one street over from Teddy. Ivette's father worked at General Motors and her mother was a third-grade teacher. They were of the social and financial ilk his mother could approve. They splurged for a grand affair to celebrate their only daughter's milestone birthday. It was his first co-ed party. His nerves were on edge until Ursula Jenkins readily befriended him. Teddy had secretly been attracted to her since junior high school, but he was too shy to ever act on his feelings.

He knew she was wearing Jean Naté. He had bought the bubble bath and body splash for his mother several times at Gray's Drug store. On his mother, it had an ordinary over-the-counter effect, while it seemed to blend effortlessly with Ursula's chemistry. He was intoxicated by her floral and citrus scent. Although he was familiar with the fragrance, it gave her an air of womanly sophistication. How she smelled that night was the second most memorable part of that night. What was most memorable was his first kiss.

"Come on Teddy. Show me your moves. I know you've got some. I'm not buying that shy act. Plus, I need somebody to dance with tonight," Ursula said pulling him out onto the makeshift dance floor, the middle of the Hamilton's posh shag-carpeted living room.

Teddy was amazed by her sudden full-on bodily attack. In moments, she had him doing the Bump, the Robot and the Errol Flynn. They melded like a dancing duo as if they were dance partners in a former life. She abruptly melted away his previous social anxiety. He was almost sure his heart leapt into the stratosphere when Ursula French kissed him while they slow danced to Gladys Knight and the Pips' soul-stirring *Best Thing That Ever Happened To Me*.

"You like that, huh?" She asked draping her arms over his shoulders. She was about a head taller than Teddy.

"Y-y-yes," he finally stammered. Her lips felt so soft. Did they taste like candy? He felt like he was dreaming. Although he was shy, he really was at a loss for words. Could she hear his heart beating? He hoped not. He had always liked Ursula because she was bubbly and full of personality. Right now, he was more enamored by her seductive aggression. He could get used to a woman taking the lead romantically.

After Ivette's party, he was being pursued by girls who had never even looked his way before. It was as if Ursula had sampled him, then spread the word that Teddy was definitely worth giving a second look. His junior and senior years at East High School, Teddy was constantly escorting classmates to homecoming, prom, and even the Starlite Cotillion. Classmates his overprotective mother never really approved of in the least. As a late bloomer, he was often surprised to be pursued by women. He never felt like he was cool, charismatic or cute. In fact, he'd often heard his peers call him a geek, nerd, or weirdo. In any case, having a listening ear and being able to carry on a decent conversation made him exceptionally attractive to the opposite sex.

His mother, however, would caution him, "All they see are your bedroom eyes. You're more than your hazel eyes Son. Don't let these girls get you caught up. You can't be falling for the okey-doke. These empty-headed girls will try to trap you. After all, I worked too hard to have you go down that path. You've got a lot more to offer than breath in britches. If you don't want to end up broken-hearted like me, then you need to demand more than a swish in a skirt." Knowing his mother's disapproval, what meager dating life Teddy had as a bachelor was generally carried on outside of their shared abode.

Chapter 2

Capital Movement

"Pardon me. Do you have these in a size seven? I like this style.   The heel is the perfect height for me," explained Elena to the saleslady in Gimbel's Department Store. She was buying a pair of Salvatore Ferragamo designer pumps to wear for her son Benjamin's upcoming wedding. His future in-laws were rich and well-known and she wanted to make a good impression. Admittedly, she was a coal miner's daughter married to a steel mill worker. However, she aimed to present herself as one of a higher, well-to-do status.

"I will go check in the back. One moment please," said the saleswoman. She reappeared with a gold embossed tissue paper lined box of the imported Italian footwear. "These are a seven. Let's see if they fit."

Elena wiggled her foot into the pump with the help of a cold shoehorn and a bit of pushing from the clerk. "Well, it's a little snug, but I think I can wear them to get some stretch. I don't want to go up a size. I'm sure my feet are just a little swollen. A few water pills will take care of that."

"Okay. I'll ring these up for you. Will that be cash or credit ma'am?"

"Credit. Here's my husband's card," she felt empowered with the plastic she used to pay. It wasn't long ago she grew up in West Virginia too poor to afford penny candy at the general store.

"Thank you for shopping at Gimbel's," said the clerk handing her the hopefully large enough shoes in a large black and white store shopping bag.

Of course, Elena had several pairs of pumps at home, yet she aimed to be dressed to perfection at Ben's wedding to

Zoe. He was marrying his college sweetheart and immediately afterwards he would begin his postgraduate studies at the Ohio State University Medical School. He was no longer temporarily in the capital city of Ohio solely for matriculation. Her married college graduate would be permanently uprooted from Harrisburg, the capital of Pennsylvania and planting new roots in Columbus with his bride. He would be a transplanted Nittany Lion practicing medicine in rival Buckeye territory.

The Eaglestons were blessed with two handsome and intelligent sons. Benjamin was accepted into the osteopathic medicine program at OSU, while his younger brother, Geraldi, was pursuing a degree in optometry at the Indiana University. Elena had wanted a larger family, but complications after delivering Gerry meant she couldn't have any more children. She always wanted a daughter. Zoe was the feminine energy she craved. Being the only woman in a household full of men overshadowed her identity outside of being a dutiful wife and doting mother.

Honestly, when Ben and Gerry went to college it had highlighted how far she and her husband, Thomas, had drifted apart from each other within their own relationship. Their livelihood was bound and tied up in the care and education of their children. Elena tried to fill her empty nest void with reading, gardening, Bingo, and Bridge parties. Thomas was so busy with work; she didn't think he even tried or needed to compensate for the fact that their sons had moved onto another life plane called adulthood. Elena knew one day they would grow up, but it seemed like it happened all too soon . . . long before she was ready.

She was daydreaming about her own wedding thirty years ago, when she was jolted back to reality by the ding of the department store elevator. There was a young, attractive Black lady aboard as the elevator attendant.

"What floor please?" she asked flashing a dynamic smile at Elena as she entered.

"Three," Elena answered tersely through partially clenched teeth. She avoided eye contact with the operator. If she had her druthers, she would avoid Colored folks altogether. There was no logical explanation for this bias, but she just didn't trust Negroes. Tapping her foot distracted Elena from seeing the polite woman standing only an arm's length away. She breathed a sigh of relief when the doors opened for her egress onto the third floor. Stepping out of the elevator car, she felt safe from any harm.

Elena went to the Millinery Department to see if she could find a hat to complement the robin's egg blue dress she would be donning as the mother of the groom. She could recall Ben directing her clearly, "Do not, and I repeat do not wear white or any shade of it on our wedding day. You cannot upstage my bride Maná."

The morning slowly drifted into afternoon and Elena was loaded down with a shopping bag of shoes, a round hat box for her new straw, sinamay, and organza hat, and a smaller bag with the least expensive bottle of Molinard Nirmala. It was all the rave. She didn't just want to look rich, she wanted to smell like luxury parfum rather than settle for drugstore eau de toilette. Thomas would be upset, but she would hide the Gimbel's account bill until after the wedding. Once he saw her vision pulled together, he wouldn't be able to complain about her spending lavishly. After all, a woman should be able to treat herself to nice things every once in a while. Right?

* * *

"Maná, what time will you and father be arriving in Columbus? We are planning to have our rehearsal dinner around 7 p.m.. Will you make it in time? I want you both there."

"Ben, of course we'll be there. I'll have your father call you later when he gets in from work with the details. We're leaving out early to get settled in our hotel. So, are you excited about the wedding? I am. I hope you're not getting cold feet," she told Ben.

"I'm leaving all the details up to Zoe. I just plan to show up," Ben admitted.

"Well, I'm sure it will be lovely," she told Ben. She wanted more details about the ceremony and reception, but since Ben had a hands-off approach to the wedding plans, she would have to live with her mounting curiosity.

The next morning, she vaguely overheard Thomas giving Ben a rundown of when they would be hitting the road to Columbus. The months in anticipation of Ben's Big Day had brought them to now being within only a few days of it actually happening.

"Don't forget to buy me a bottle of DeWitt's pills on your way home. I'm holding in a little water weight that I need to shed before Ben's wedding," she added as Thomas headed off to his last day of work before the grand nuptials. She handed him his lunch pail and Thermos. She gave what he expected. It was a part of their couple routine. She prayed Ben and Zoe would find joy in their marriage. As long as you give your partner whatever they expected, that was a keeping force.

Chapter 3

You Can't Do Anything Right

"**T**eddy! Teddy! Wake up! I need you to go to the store," Thelma banged on the staircase wall with her wooden spoon. She knew he loved to sleep in on the weekends, but she was out of her beloved Balmoral cigarettes. She desperately needed her dose of tar-laced nicotine.

"Ma, can't you just leave me alone? I was having the best dream," Teddy rolled over trying to block out her pounding racket.

"Go to the store and I will leave you alone. I need cigarettes. We need food. I need to start tomorrow's dinner."

Teddy had grown up with his mother's many idiosyncrasies. Preparing her Sunday dinner on Saturday was just one of them. He wondered why his mother even bothered to prepare their meal a day early, because they never went to church. When he asked her why she always made Sunday's meal a day earlier, she told him that's how her mother always did it. Apparently, Grandma Bailey, a day laborer who cleaned in White folks' homes, had to do most of her own cooking and cleaning on the weekends. In order to give herself a bit of a break, Grandma would fix a big dinner on Saturday and rest up on Sunday before having to travel across town to report for duty as a domestic.

"Okay. Okay, Ma. I'm coming down in a few minutes," he told his impatient mother.

"Here's my list. Now read it back to me. You always forget something. Maybe if you hear it and see it, then you won't forget or mess it up," Thelma offered.

"Cigarettes, cornstarch, Kotex. Eww," he paused and frowned in requisite masculine disgust. "Eggs, milk, butter . . ." he read the list back to her slowly.

"Real butter. Not that margarine or oleo that flies won't even land on."

"Hamburger, whole chicken, pot roast, celery, carrots, potatoes."

"Make sure they say 'from Idaho' on the bag. I don't want no hot house potatoes or tomatoes," Thelma instructed.

Teddy let out a heavy sigh. "Onions, green pepper, corn on the cob, heavy cream, crackers and raisins," he finished the recital of an all too familiar grocery list.

"Don't get heavy whipping cream this time just heavy cream. Read the carton for goodness' sakes. Don't forget to take them pop bottles back either," Thelma charged.

He couldn't help but notice her primary focus was for her precious cigarettes and her pica craving, Argo cornstarch. There was some psychology behind Thelma's addictions involving oral fixation. Teddy didn't subscribe to nor care about the scientific mumbo jumbo; he just wished his mother would magically be rid of these vile habits. He also despised his role as being her enabler. But what choice did he have other than to placate her?

"I don't know if I like the new neighbor lady. She dresses funny. All those head turbans, bangles, and baptism clothes," Thelma observed.

"Baptism clothes?"

"Yes, we used to have to wear wrapped robes like she does when we got baptized in the river. I don't know where she shops, but I bet somewhere a church is missing their baptism gowns."

"You must mean Miss Ouida?

"Is that her name? Weed what?"

"Ouida. It's a Creole name. She's good people. She's Mr. Bennett's sister. She is taking care of him."

"Humph. That's what she told you. She probably just came to take all his money and get that house," Thelma scoffed.

"Really Ma? I don't know how you would come to that conclusion. You haven't even met her."

"I don't need to meet her. I know people. I know she didn't just suddenly move here purely out of the goodness of her heart. She's getting something out of the deal. They don't even look alike. How do you know that's his *real* sister?" Thelma said raising her eyebrow as she questioned Teddy.

"Ma, you sit in that window all day and have an overactive imagination."

"She's always feeding the pigeons. Why, I'll never know. If you feed pigeons, then expect pigeon poop."

"Ma, I don't have time to debate about the sanity or lunacy of bird feeding. I'm going to the store. Bye." Teddy left out to fulfill Thelma's marketplace wishlist.

* * *

Fortunately, Teddy and Thelma didn't live far from the Greenway Avenue Kroger. He loaded up the empty glass pop bottles. He had to return them to get back the nickel per bottle deposit money they had paid. Every week he and his mother both consumed an eight pack a piece of soda or as most born and bred Buckeyes called it "pop". His favorite was A&W Root beer and hers was Pepsi.

As soon as he walked in, he saw his newfound crush, Angela Gonzalez. She was so bashful and he liked winking at her to make her blush. Once he had shopped for his mother's extensive list, he made a bee line to her lane for checkout.

"Hi Teddy. Do you have any coupons today?" she asked while her cheeks became rosy red from embarrassment.

"No. I don't." This was part of the game they played. Angela pulled out a small metal file box from under her register and began searching for coupons to help Teddy save on his food bill. She found one for eggs, meat, the crackers, raisins and even the

Kotex his mother needed.

"These should help," she rang up his entire order then deducted the coupons. "That will be $37.15."

"That's all? I'll have enough to take you out on a date. When are you going to give me your number, Sweetness?"

"Teddy, you know I can't do that. Company policy," she whispered in protest as she leaned closer to him over the moving conveyor belt.

"Agh! You break my heart," he clutched at his chest and feigned great disappointment. Maybe one day he could get her to bend the rules a little bit and give up her digits. For now, he enjoyed their innocent flirtatious banter.

He went back home and unloaded all of the groceries. Of course, Thelma had to find fault.

"Where are my cigarettes? And why did you get Clabber Girl instead of Argo cornstarch? Why did you get the California raisins instead of the generic black and white ones?"

"Ma! Gimme a break. I'm going right back out to get your Balmorals. They didn't have Argo, so Clabber Girl will have to do for now. Plus, the clerk hooked me up with a coupon for the name brand raisins," explained a frustrated Teddy.

"You can't do anything right! You make me sick," Thelma continued to complain.

"I can't take this anymore!" he said slamming the side door and heading to his car. He wasn't sure where exactly he was going, but he had to put a good amount of distance between him and his nagging mother rather quickly.

"**L**egacy is about what you teach, not always about what you gave."

~Malcolm "MJ" Harris ♥

Chapter 4

Private Practice Versus Franchisee

The Greek Orthodox faith held a strong biblical belief that one should leave an inheritance or blessing to their children's children. Papa Eagleston, the paternal grandfather, had left quite a substantial sum to his grandchildren particularly his grandsons Benjamin and Geraldi. The patriarch probably had no idea he would be leaving both with the much-needed seed money to start their own private practices. The money set the brothers up royally.

"Zoe, I have to leave now. I'm supposed to meet with the architect on the final design for the medical building. I don't want to be late," Ben said hurriedly eating his breakfast scone. As soon as the estate of Papa Eagleston released the lionshare of his inheritance, Ben got to work on finding a place where he could hang his shingle, 'Dr. Benjamin O. Eagleston, D. O.'. He wanted to be his own boss and no longer be under the University and its strict protocols and time-consuming demands. He knew every year as an OSU employee, he was parting with money that could be lining his own pockets instead of the hospital's coffers. He had chosen his specialty in osteopathy because it was a lucrative line of work where he could earn more than six times that of a mere medical doctor.

"Honey, you said the meeting is at 10:00 a.m., but it's only eight o'clock now," said Zoe who hated to see Ben work himself into a frenzy needlessly. She had learned her husband was driven, headstrong and competitive. Once he was on a roll there was no stopping him.

"I want to make sure I'm there, waiting, and in position. If this deal falls apart, it won't be on my end."

"I'm sure you've dotted all your i's and crossed all your t's. Relax.

You've got this."

"I adore you my Belladonna. I'll see you this evening. Enjoy your day," he left giving her a kiss on the cheek on his way to his prospective architect's office.

Ben headed across town to meet with his future medical building's architect. The structure was simple enough with office space, a waiting area, patient rooms and an onsite lab. His practice was going to be the first of its kind on the west side of town. Most doctors tended to steer clear of setting up shop in the underserved area mistakenly believing they would not be able to maintain a thriving financially viable practice there. Ben knew otherwise. He had kept his ear to the ground and knew about programs outside of Medicaid and Medicare that could funnel money into urban areas in need of quality public health. His plan to be on the west side was indeed strategic.

Ben pulled into the parking lot of Executive Office Space on East Broad Street. Only a handful of cars were there. It was barely half past eight, so he knew his only option was to wait. He checked himself in the rearview mirror. He made sure his bushy eyebrows weren't looking untamed. He sprayed some peppermint Binaca in his mouth and adjusted his tie. That took less than three minutes. He wasn't sure if he should wait in his car or head inside. He didn't want to seem overly eager or pushy, but he also didn't want anyone thinking he was some random weird loitering lurker either. At 9:15, he couldn't postpone the inevitable . . . going inside.

To his surprise, the staff was all relatively young Black people. The receptionist, the secretary, and all the other people he seen there filing in and out of offices. He was directed to wait in the conference room for Mr. Bacardi.

"Hello," Ben heard a powerful voice approaching from behind. He swiveled around in his high back chair to face his chosen architect, Mr. Bacardi. To his surprise, Mr. Bacardi was a middle-aged Black man. For whatever reason, Ben had mistakenly assumed Bacardi was an Italian name.

"Good morning, Sir. Great to finally meet you," he managed to proclaim even though he never considered working with a minority. He collected his thoughts and briefed Bacardi on his vision for his medical center.

Bacardi was thoroughly above board and professional. He took Ben to a completed light brick stand-alone facility nearby that was akin to the one he wanted built. Satisfied with Bacardi's caliber of work, Ben filled out the preliminary paperwork for a contract to build. He left satisfied knowing that in roughly eighteen months, barring any major snafus, he would be opening his very own freestanding medical suite in the west side Hilltop area.

* * *

Geraldi was the antithesis of his older brother Ben. He was a family man first and physician second. Actually, he was an optometrist which Ben often chided him wasn't a real doctor. He ignored Ben and his superiority complex. When Papa Eagleston passed, Gerry was more practical with his money. He was married with three children, but made a decent salary to live comfortably working as a teaching and practicing optometrist for Ohio State. Since he wanted to be able to pass on the tradition of providing for his children's children, he placed the majority of his inheritance into an annuity that would be worth a lot more once it matured. His motivation was being intentional with longevity and legacy. He was consciously building a nest egg for his golden retirement and for his children.

"Gerry, did you know the architect you referred me to was Black?" Ben asked on the phone.

"No. Should it matter?" Gerry replied staunchly.

"I guess not. I just thought Bacardi was an Italian name. You don't know of any architects in our church family? I feel like I'm letting a lot of money escape *our* community, if you know what I mean."

"I think I understand your meaning and it's foolishness Ben! We're all one race, the human race, under our skin. Have you ever seen a White cadaver that was markedly different from a Black one? No, you haven't. So, if Bacardi is a licensed and learned man, then he should be suitable for the job. Lest you forget the prejudice our grandparents and parents endured as immigrants. Sometimes I find it hard to believe we grew up in the same household together."

"I just want to be deliberate with my investment. That's all."

"Being intentional about whom you deal with is one thing, but discrimination is entirely another thing. If you see a future working only with people who look like you, you're sadly disillusioned. Grow up Ben! Times have changed. You need to roll with the punches and get with the program."

Chapter 5

The Weird Lady Next Door

"Teddy, please come home right after work. I don't want to be here by myself. You can pass out the candy. You always seem to have fun doing it," Thelma asked a distracted Teddy.

"It's not so much I enjoy it, but you refuse to do it," Teddy responded flatly. His recollection was that Halloween or Beggar's Night was an odd observance in the Robinson household. He was never allowed to go trick or treating like the other children in Eastgate. His mother told him when he was about three years old, the very first year he went out as a clown, a prankster placed a fish head in his plastic orange and black jack o'lantern bucket. She vowed never to take him out again. Thelma didn't actively celebrate the pagan observance again until Teddy became a teenager. She began passing out Tootsie rolls and Dum-Dum suckers because of a handwritten complaint. Apparently, a young neighbor felt compelled to leave a notebook paper notice written in crayon warning her that her car and house would be egged if no sweet treats were provided. The anonymous ghost or goblin even drew a skull and crossbones on the makeshift manifesto. Teddy wished he knew the juvenile mastermind of the note. It was an effective message because every year since Thelma ensured there was some token of sweetness to offer the trick or treaters who came to their door.

"What are you giving out this year?"

"You remember. I got those bags of discounted Easter candy. I'm not going broke to satisfy these ghoulish goons," Thelma boasted of her money-saving scheme.

"I hope they don't mind almost six-month-old candy," Teddy shaking his head at his mother who was proud to be a consummate penny pincher.

"Hmph. I'm on a fixed income. That's all I got. They'll take it or leave it."

"Well, if I take a half hour for lunch, I can leave at four thirty and be home by five. Okay?" he asked.

"Fine."

* * *

Teddy had gone to the store to grab a bag of individually-wrapped miniature packs of Now and Laters and a bag of Hershey kisses. He couldn't in good conscience pass out candy he considered too old to eat himself to innocent and unsuspecting children.

He pulled into their driveway and Thelma was at her familiar perch at the kitchen bay window. It was a little past five because he had made the one unplanned stop. "Have they been here?"

"No. No one has come by yet. I think it's not supposed to start until six anyway."

"Good," he said and emptied the newly purchased candy on top of the offerings Thelma had arranged in a large pastel yellow, pink and green straw Easter basket. She had absolutely no shame.

They waited. No visitors.

At one point, he heard the faint giggles of children. They went to Mr. Bennett's house. So, Teddy knew soon they would be knocking at their door.

No one ever came.

Again, he heard footsteps rustling over fall leaves. He figured whomever was walking out there would make their way over as soon as they hit up Mr. Bennett for candy.

This time he witnessed children running and screaming in the other direction. No laughter. Just terror. Teddy was a bit alarmed. He knew Mr. Bennett was ill. He wondered what could have happened to make these kids flee so quickly. He put on his jacket to investigate the goings on next door.

He knocked. No immediate answer, but he could hear movement and eerie music from behind the door.

"Mr. Bennett are you alright? Miss Ouida are you okay?" The door swung open and there was Ouida. Teddy let out a high-pitched scream. Ouida had a plastic ax in her hand she had smeared with some congealed substance that looked like blood on it. Her white hair was teased up all over her head into a something that resembled a bird's nest with tendrils. She had on a butcher's smock type coat covered with streaks of the fake blood. Her eyes were her scariest feature. Somehow, she had silver and white pupil contact lenses that gave her a realistic other worldly look. The only thing amateurish about her daunting disguise was her plastic glow in the dark fangs.

"I'm okay," said Ouida howling with laughter. "I really had you. You should see your face right now. I'm just having a little fun with the kids."

"Man! You scared me and I'm a grown man," Teddy said breathlessly. He wasn't too happy that Ouida was relishing in his fearful reaction.

"Okay. I'm sorry. I tricked you, would you like a treat?"

"No. We've got candy at home next door."

Ouida placed one hand on her hip and the other on the front door frame as she leaned forward and told Teddy, "I wasn't talking about candy."

"Oh well. I don't want to miss any trick or treaters," said Teddy catching her unwelcomed romantic drift. He walked hurriedly back to his post at home. He wanted to erase this new Halloween memory from his bruised psyche forever.

Chapter 6

Bamboozled

I t was payday Friday. Teddy was dressed in his flyest pick-me-tonight outfit and ready to go cut a rug at Papa Jack's nightclub downtown. He would rather go on Thursday which was Ladies' Night. The extended happy hour on Thursdays saved Teddy immensely. He was not as smooth as most, so plying women with hard liquor and wine was his lead magnet. Once a fine female specimen had been reeled in so to speak, then he tried to dazzle them with his conversation and charm.

Teddy walked in the club and headed straight for the bar. He needed a double dose of liquid courage . . . a double shot of Hennessy. There went five dollars. He needed to pace himself or his entertainment budget for the night would quickly evaporate.

"Hello Handsome. You don't look familiar. I'm Ranessa. Nice to meet you," said a curvy sepia tone foxy lady extending her dainty hand towards him.

"Thanks for the compliment. I'm Teddy. Nice to meet you. Would you like a drink pretty lady?" he offered hoping it was one drink that she sipped slowly. Being a gentleman sometimes cost him mad bread when his potential paramours could double fist beers or nearly drink him under the table.

"Sure. I'll have Sex on the Beach please," she directed the bartender without batting an eye.

"That's a drink?" Teddy scoffed. He was extremely green to the bar scene.

"Well, I would hope so since there aren't many beaches around here unless you count Alum Creek beach," she laughed at his sincere question.

"I guess technically the area along the shore of a body of water is a beach, but I think of oceanfront beaches as *real* beaches. Alum Creek doesn't even register."

"Okay. Okay. Let's not be so technical. Other than bars or beaches, where do you like to hang out or just chill?" Ranessa asked gingerly touching the glass of her colorful drink. Teddy was mesmerized by her gaze. Her direct focus on him made him weak. Most women, especially the beautiful unobtainable types, wanted to talk about themselves, their past failed relationships, their problems or their feelings. In this brief encounter, she surprised him by wanting to get to know about him . . . the real Teddy.

"I'm really a quiet guy. I like nature. Walking, skiing, jogging . . . just about any outdoor activity I love. When I have time, I enjoy birdwatching. What about you? Do you come here a lot? You said you didn't recognize me."

"Well, I don't get out much, but when I do, this is my go-to spot. It's close to home. Besides, it's my kinda crowd. My kinda people," she playfully slapped Teddy on the thigh. Perhaps she was trying to verify if he was the physically fit outdoorsman he claimed to be.

"How about we hang out on the dance floor for a bit? They're playing my song," Teddy suggested. While he was adept at small talk, he wanted to move away from the bar to avoid running up a huge tab. The DJ had *Celebrate Good Times* by Kool & the Gang blaring. He wanted to see if foxy Ranessa had any sly moves. Smooth moves he hoped she might be putting on him later for a really good time.

The two danced together for several songs. When a slow jam played, Teddy was ready to rest, but Ranessa coaxed him into swaying and swooning to Roberta Flack's *The First Time Ever I Saw Your Face*. He held her close and the lyrics transfixed him to another place. The slow mellow ballad was speaking to him. He felt so relaxed with Ranessa in his arms who seemed so in control of this intimate moment. Why did God make her so soft and sweet-smelling like a rose? Although she was an acquaintance of only a few hours, he felt like they had been romantically linked for decades. Was his mind playing tricks on him? Or perhaps his tender heart was the culprit? Or maybe another part of his anatomy was taking over him?

"Well, I think we should get some fresh air. What do you say?"

"I'm down," he replied eagerly. Maybe Ranessa was amped for some quickie action in his car. She struck him as pretty bold. Maybe she was freaky too.

They stopped at the pay stand to get their hands stamped for reentry. He didn't want to repay the $10 cover charge for himself nor the $5 for her.

"Where's your car? My feet hurt," she asked as soon as they escaped into the cool night air.

"I'm parked across the street," he said. The low lights inside the club did not do Ranessa justice. She was an ebony beauty from head to toe. She had flawless skin and a Coke bottle shape that her dress clung to effortlessly. He wanted to be that dress hugging her curves.

He opened the passenger side door for her. She complimented him for being such a gentleman. He proceeded to enter on the driver's side.

"Do you mind if I take off my shoes?" she asked as soon as he shut his door.

He did mind, but still anticipating getting to know her better he said, "No". Something about people taking their shoes off always made him think he was smelling corn chips.

"Good," she said wincing as she slid her platform cork-heeled shoes off. "You smoke?" she offered him a cigarette.

"No." He wanted to say how much he thought smoking was not ladylike and the smell repulsed him. Why hadn't he noticed the smell of smoke on her earlier? They had danced with one another, but when you're in a smoke-filled room, you can't attribute the stale smell of the cancer sticks to one particular person. He was obviously too fixated on other things. Like now, despite the possibility of it being like licking an ashtray, he was overly anxious to kiss her.

She lit up and took a long drag. "Look, I like to be up front and honest with all my Johns. It's 100 for a fifty fifty and 200 for all the way. Five hundred for the night at your place. I've got six kids and I like to keep them out of my business. You dig?"

"Wait? What? You're a ho? A prostitute?" he was shocked. He leaned away from her pressing his back firmly against his car door. It was a wonder it didn't pop open from all the pressure he was applying. Being mistaken for a paying customer had never happened to him. He was used to getting the drawls for free.

"That's minus the motel. You got I.D.? Condoms?"

"What? Are you serious? You can get the hell out of my car lady. I'm nobody's John," he said angrily while he leaned over her to open her car door.

"Okay. Don't get all bent outta shape Fella. I kinda like you Teddy. You got me kinda hot and bothered, I ain't gonna lie. We can split the motel. I'll do you for free . . . a little sample to get you hooked," she winked. "You'll bring me back here afterwards and I can at least score one paid gig tonight."

"Get out!" he pointed for her to exit his vehicle. He was upset and mortified that he had been duped, hoodwinked, and bamboozled.

"Well can I at least get a ride home? I took the bus here. I'll even let you come in for a nightcap. On the house of course because you are fine baby," she said still trying to bait Teddy onto her sexual string seductively.

"Please just get out. You've already wasted my time and money," said a disappointed Teddy.

"Well, hell, you've cost me time and money too. You damned jive turkey! You cheap ass prick!" Ranessa said loudly slamming his car door.

He started his car and let it warm up while he watched his dream turned nightmare lady wobble barefoot back into the club. He was grateful she hadn't weaponized her clunky shoes after he flat out rejected her solicitation. Once he saw she had returned safely to the club, he turned out of the lot and headed home.

Chapter 7

Can We Talk?

Teddy woke up with a hellacious hangover. He went downstairs to see if eating might lessen his painful headache.

"Teddy. Tie my shoe," ordered Thelma plopping her foot on the kitchen chair for him to tie her shoelace.

"Can I just come down and eat my frosted flakes in peace before you start with the 'Teddy do this or Teddy do thats'? I had a terrible night. I need a little time and space to recuperate."

"So that's my fault?"

"I didn't say that Ma. But where are you going? You can't sit there with your shoes untied? Where are your house shoes?"

"Do I have to be going somewhere? I let you sleep in today being that it's Saturday. But if tying my shoe is too much for you, then I won't bother you," she said lowering her foot.

He hated when she tried to guilt trip him into doing things for her. He didn't mind helping his mother. It just seemed like the more he gave into her frivolous demands she continued full throttle with even more commands to do menial tasks. If he didn't honor her requests, then he was being a bad son. He couldn't win. He filled the tea kettle and sat with her at the kitchen table. As soon as he plopped down, she jumped up.

"There he is," said an almost giddy Thelma. Loose shoes and all she glided to their front door. The postman was walking up to their porch to deliver the mail.

Teddy was not believing this persona of the woman he called mother who greeted the mailman.

"Good afternoon, Mrs. Robinson. Sorry I am running behind

today. I left the station a little late. Someone called off sick, so the mail for my route wasn't ready," he said flashing a toothy grin.

"Well, you're here now. And it's Miss. I'm widowed. Actually, you can call me Thelma," she said tacitly informing him about her marital status.

"Ma'am, I just want to be respectful to my elders."

Teddy tried hard to hold in his laughter. All of a sudden she wasn't simply a divorcee, but a widow no doubt. Maybe she was trying to beguile him with a sympathy angle. His mother was shamelessly flirting, but her romantic target basically had just called her old. He went to move the kettle off the fire. His hot water was ready for his cereal. He was lactose intolerant so he doused his morning bowl of grains with hot water and ate it like mush.

"I'm not that old Mack," defeated by his conclusion that she was his elder rather than his peer.

"I hate to give you these, but they belong to you," Mack handed her a stack of letters. "Bills I presume," he chuckled.

"Thanks. See you on Monday," she waved as he walked away to the next house.

"So that's who you were tying your cute pink shoes for Mom?"

"Oh, please Teddy. I just get the mail so people don't think no one is home if it's left sitting in the box," Thelma tried to explain. She was a terrible liar.

"Like they couldn't see you sitting in the window and instantly deduce that information? You've got a crush on the mailman. I hope it's just a crush. What happens when I am not here?" he said poking around in his cooling breakfast.

"Don't question me. I don't question you about your love interests."

"So, it is more than a crush. Mack the mailman is your love interest. Wow. Does he know that you two are lovebirds? Seems like he thinks you're a little old lady Mrs. Robinson."

Knock. Knock. Again, someone was at their door. It was a needed interruption to their awkward exchange.

"I think this is yours," said Ouida handing Thelma a piece of mail that had been misdelivered.

"Thank you," said Thelma trying to shut the door.

"I'm sorry. But can I borrow Teddy for a minute? I need the light over the back door replaced," Ouida had managed to place a portion of her body in the doorway so Ouida couldn't immediately dismiss her like she usually did.

"Oh sure. I'll go get him."

"Tell her I'm coming. I just need to put on a shirt first."

"She heard you. Don't be long. I need you to go to the store. I've got to get tomorrow's dinner started.

"It can't take long to change a light bulb. I'll be right back," Teddy reassured an impatient Thelma.

He walked around to Mr. Bennett's backyard. "Do you have a ladder? I can't quite reach that," he craned his head upward trying yet failing to reach the bad bulb.

"I think there's a ladder in the shed."

He walked over to the tool shed at the fence line. "It's padlocked. Do you have the key?"

"No. Freddie has it with him. There's no telling when he'll be back. I didn't think it was too high for you to reach. Come on inside. I can at least make you some fresh lemonade for your trouble," Ouida offered.

He didn't want to be rude and refuse her hospitality, so he followed her into the kitchen.

Ouida grabbed the pitcher, lemons, ice and the sugar canister to make her special concoction. "Sit down. Let me talk to you before you take off."

"Okay, wassup?" He obliged and plopped down on a tall kitchen stool. Watching her make the lemonade made him wonder why his mother had never made old-fashioned lemonade from scratch. "I want to give you a bit of advice. I wish someone had told me this when I was your age."

He gave her a quizzical look.

"See all my life I have been taking care of people. My parents were sickly, my husbands weren't well either, and now my brother. I don't mind. But I am an old woman now and not once did anybody ever tell me to take a break and just live my life for me. If I was not changing sheets, dumping bed pans, or dressing wounds for somebody, then I felt lost. I think you young people call it finding yourself."

Teddy nodded as if he understood, but he wasn't exactly receiving the pearl of wisdom she was trying to convey to him.

"I consider my caregiving a labor of love. Forgive me when I say this, but you taking care of your mother seems different. You're tied to your mother from obligation. I don't see you with friends your own age. How are you going to live your life if you're wrapped up, tied up, and tangled up in forever being a mama's boy? I'm not saying you need to quit doing things for you mother, but don't forget to live YOUR life along the way. Don't end up like me with more days behind you than ahead of you without a life well-lived. Are you understanding me?"

"I think so."

"So, the next time I see you, I pray you'll have a smile on your face. I mean no harm, but you look miserable all the time. When do you get out and just have fun? Bennett says all you do is work and look after your mother. I'll sit with her or help you out. As a young man, you need to be out exploring the world and finding what makes you tick. She's never going to cut you loose from her apron strings. Bennett says you're gunho about birds. You ever wonder why you've never left the nest? You're grown. You're college educated. You're not sickly. All hallmarks that say you can fly on your own. She's comfortable and may never feel you're ready to leave the nest. You're going to have to just free yourself. Understand?"

"Yes," he was beginning to process her concern. It was a fact he struggled with for years. The obvious being highlighted by someone relatively new to him was confirmation that the Teddy and Thelma dynamic wasn't ideal. Knowing that and purposely changing his current situation would be easier said than done. He'd promised his mother he would not be long. He stood up to leave, but Ouida grabbed him unexpectedly by his forearm.

"Why are you in such a hurry to leave?"

It was as if she already knew he felt duty-bound to return home quickly. "Well, I need to get home and do some shopping for Mom," he said sheepishly.

"You're a hard nut to crack. Can't we sit and enjoy a casual conversation without you worrying about your mother like she's going to fall to pieces if you leave her alone for more than fifteen minutes? Here just sit a spell with me. Consider it your first act of rebellion on the road to claim your independence," Ouida handed him a glass of lemonade.

"I guess you're right," Teddy said sitting back down on the red padded kitchen stool. He took in several gulps of the ice-cold lemonade. "Let me ask you a question."

"Alright, what is it?"

"Why do you hang those empty glass bottles on the tree branches? Are they some type of decorations?"

"Oh, I thought you had a hard question. Those are to collect any evil spirits before they enter the house. My mother always did it. When I first arrived here my brother Freddie was deathly ill. Shortly after I hung the spirit catchers, his health started improving. Now he's all better and spending more time with his ladyfriend. Not too many people believe in that type of thing anymore. It may seem silly to some, but I still do what works for me."

"Oh, I see," said Teddy. He had been intrigued by the colorful display ever since Ouida started placing clear, amber, green red, and blue glass bottles on the thicker tree branches of Mr. Bennett's hawthorn tree.

"Me, I'm just a country girl at heart. I remember one summer we had to chalk the well. Technically, Freddie had to help my dad and I didn't wanna be left behind doing girly things. I guess I thought I might miss out on something. I ended up being overcome by the fumes from the process. That's when I learned I had asthma. That's when I found out how much my big brother really loved me."

"Daddy stayed with me at the well while Freddy ran back to the house like lightning to get help. That chemical exposure damaged my asthmatic lungs. For weeks, Freddie catered to my every whim. In a way, he was my first role model in caregiving. That well accident cemented our bond as brother and sister. There's nothing I wouldn't do for him and him for me. You dig?"

Teddy nodded. She poured him another glass of lemonade. Apparently, she had more to say.

"You think I'm a little off my rocker don't you?" Ouida leaned towards him to examine his body language for truthfulness.

"No ma'am. I wouldn't say that. It's just that my mother doesn't particularly care for you. Truthfully, I don't think she cares for anybody."

"What do *you* think about me?"

"Well, you did scare the Bejesus outta me on Beggars' Night," he admitted. They both laughed.

"You should have seen your face," she said then tried to regain her earnest composure. "I'm sorry about that night. I also hope I didn't scare you thinking I was the dirty old lady next door. I was just funning with you. My romantic days are over. I had to string six men together to try to make one decent husband. Now love and stuff isn't in the cards for me. Lord knows I tried. I gave up. What about you? You got a special young lady in your life?"

"No ma'am. I don't." Considering his brief encounter with Ranessa the night before, he wasn't sure if his love life or the lack of one was a topic he cared to discuss with Ouida. He couldn't help but think she was reading his mind.

"Well, I won't pry. I just think a nice handsome young man like you, with a nice job, a decent car and most importantly a kind heart would be a great catch. Teddy, you come by here and bend my ear anytime. You live right next door so there's no need to be a stranger. Come by anytime," she said.

Teddy left feeling like he was on a mission. He had a brand-new homework assignment. His next-door neighbor reached out and challenged him. He was to find and do what made him happy. Why? Because Miss Ouida had told him to.

Chapter 8

A Change Is Gonna Come

"Teddy, I can't believe this," said Thelma in a worried tone. She was tapping her left leg uncontrollably. Her fidgeting was a clear sign that she was worked up in a tizzy over something. Her lips wrapped over her teeth as she was plunged into deep disturbing thought.

"Believe what Ma? What is it now?" Teddy grew weary over Thelma and all the trivial things she made into insurmountable mountains. The last critical issue was the giant sinkhole in front of the downtown Palace Theatre. Something that had absolutely nothing to do with her. She rarely left the house anymore. She didn't drive because Teddy chauffeured her to any of her medical appointments, the sole reason she left home nowadays. The City's downtown area was definitely not her scene. So when would she be in danger of being swallowed up by a faltering pavement crater? In all honesty, Teddy felt like Thelma enjoyed inserting herself into the far-out scenarios she read about in the *Columbus Dispatch* or heard on the local television news.

"This announcement from the Eastgate Civic Association," Thelma waved a canary yellow page that read "NOTICE" towards him.

"Civic association? I didn't know we had one," Teddy took the flyer from her to see what exactly had triggered her anxiety.

"There's a meeting next week about the new freeway that's slated to come right through here. They're going to build a connector between downtown and the airport. I can't do this again," she said putting her coffee mug down a little more forcefully than either of them expected.

"Again? What do you mean?"

"This is the Flytown debacle all over again. The City decided the exact spot where our family home was situated should be an interstate." Thelma's voice was shaky as she began crying. "They didn't care. They just came in and wiped out the only place I had ever called home. I was only nine at the time. My parents weren't rich and we never had much, but the powers that be saw fit to come and take away what little we had. I'm on a fixed income. I can't afford to be uprooted like that again. I can't. I won't. You're taking me to that meeting. We're going to fight this!"

"Hold on. We? Why we?" Teddy was seeing the freeway project as a valid reason to finally part ways with his needy and overbearing mother. Whenever he tried to discuss moving out on his own, she went into a depressive tailspin. Thelma behaved as if she was a frail woman who would be dead within a week if he left her alone and unprotected. She would lavish Teddy with gifts to entice him to stay. Her manipulation was shameless, but it worked. To keep Teddy by her side, he lived with her rent free, she paid his car note and car insurance. Teddy put up with the collateral toxicity of their set up. By saving money on his primary necessities, shelter and transportation, Teddy could then afford to spend his money frivolously.

"Teddy, we have to get involved. I just hope it's not too late. People mistakenly think these officials, city planners, or politicians are looking out for our best interests. Sadly, we don't get involved until we've got some skin in the game. I'm pretty sure our tiny house being bulldozed for a freeway counts as skin in the game. Don't you agree?"

"Yeah, I see your point."

"Make me a fresh pot of coffee," Thelma ordered. Rarely did she bother to give Teddy the courtesy of saying "please" and "thank you" as she required of him. Even as an adult child, he had to mind his manners, while she as a parent did not. In her book, respect was never a two-way but always a one-way street.

"What's wrong with what's in here? Teddy asked holding up a

half full carafe.

"Teddy, just make me a new pot," she replied rudely.

"I don't know why you drink this swill and without cream and sugar no doubt."

"Just make me the darn coffee. No need for your peanut gallery commentary."

The scared Thelma who moments earlier was vulnerable and fearful of losing her adulthood home had easily morphed back into the bristling and demanding shrew he tolerated for free room and board. He was positive he wouldn't let any other woman treat him so poorly. Teddy cowered in order to keep the peace between them. He wished he had enough fortitude to walk away and quit playing this cruel game.

Chapter 9

An Edifice In Danger

"When is this supposed to happen?" Asked Howard Growlin the church custodian. He was actually the groundskeeper, the handyman, and the tale bearer of all news good and bad about the parishioners of the Greek Reclamation Church. His wife, Cora, had the market cornered on all the juicy gossip tidbits that floated around about the congregation.

"Well, we don't have a specific time frame as yet. We're going to the next city planning meeting to garner more information. They've offered us a million dollars for the property which is ludicrous. This building nor the land attached to it is for sale. It is holy ground," said Metropolitan Parelli. He had been at the helm of the orthodox Greek parish for thirty years.

"Exactly who is going to this planning meeting? Besides yourself, who can adequately represent our church's stance?" Asked Deacon Sideris.

"It will be myself, Father Constantine and Michael Bezik. He's an attorney well versed in corporate and real estate law," replied Metropolitan Parelli. He anticipated this line of questioning, but he still found it annoying. Continually answering to the scrutinizing laity consumed a majority of his time. It was precious time wasted that he could otherwise dedicate to more fruitful activities within the parish.

"How was this lawyer chosen? His surname doesn't sound familiar." Sideris crossed his arms awaiting an answer. There were about fifty families represented within the Reclamation Church. Longstanding members recognized each other by their family name. Someone with an unfamiliar name would need to be connected in some way to a member in good standing as a means of vetting them to gain the trust or respect of the tight knit religious group.

"He comes highly recommended by Dominic Papadopoulos. He's been a member here for about twenty years. You might remember I married his daughter last summer." The men began nodding to acknowledge familiarity with the Papadopoulos clan. They were older members who weren't active in the traditional sense of attending services or observing the sacraments, but they were charter members of the Reclamation church body nonetheless.

"Aren't there repairs in excess of a million dollars to be performed here? The Church desperately needs a new roof. We can't just cut our losses and move to a more modern building in the suburbs? No offense to you Growlin, but you're getting up in age and the upkeep of these premises can be challenging and overwhelming for you, right?" Deacon Sideris asked.

Growlin didn't appreciate Sideris' assessment of his ability or inability to render adequate custodial services. "I do alright. I manage," he said flatly in a brooding tone. His face turning crimson from being called out directly. This was not the first time he was openly criticized about his job as the janitor. As he aged, complaints about him far outnumbered compliments for him. It seemed like par for the course.

"As I stated before, this church is situated on hallowed ground. We will not sell and we will not be moved. If the National Church Council needs to be involved that will be our next level course of action," Metropolitan reiterated to the concerned faces before him. "Growlin your position here is safe and secure. I can personally guarantee that," he added trying to unruffle Growlin's feathers. His authoritative tone clarified his staunch position.

A look of satisfaction appeared over Growlin's sallow face. If Metropolitan had his back, then he had absolutely nothing to worry about. He squared his shoulders and sat up a little straighter feeling fully supported by his immediate boss.

"We'll adjourn today's meeting. I caution you that nothing discussed here today leaves this room. This is Church business and I want to keep it that way. Remember your solemn oath to the Elder Council. Please enjoy the light refreshments available in the fellowship hall. Have a safe trip home gentlemen," Metropolitan announced before concluding their meeting with prayer. If the Reclamation Church was to remain, then they would need divine intervention to do so.

Chapter 10

Time for Anger Management

One thing Teddy could appreciate about Gail Evans was that she was a fair boss. He didn't always agree with how she ran the department, but for the most part, to him, she was fair.

"Well, Teddy, I'm pretty sure you can figure out why I have called you in here today?" Gail looked at him sternly. He didn't know if he was just in trouble or deep deep trouble.

"It's probably about the exchange I had with Bernadine last week while you were out."

"Indeed, it is," she said waving a handwritten form he assumed Bernadine had filled out after the incident. Bernadine was an older file clerk in their department who was set in her ways. She didn't like the fact that Teddy would only use interoffice envelopes once or twice. Instead of recycling them, Teddy was constantly ordering new ones. His numerous supply orders thus required her to complete a purchase order and then deliver said envelopes to Teddy. While Gail was out, Bernadine seized the opportunity to confront him with this trivial matter.

"What's her side of the story?"

"In a nutshell, she said you cussed her out Teddy. Is that true?"

"She asked me not to submit so many requests for office supplies. Which considering she is the unit file clerk, fulfillment is clearly in her purview, I thought it was a ridiculous and unnecessary request. I may have called her an old bitty and told her to leave me the hell alone and just do her effing job. That's my edited version."

"Honestly, I'm disappointed in both of you. I leave for one week, five whole business days, and this is the turmoil I get to address when I return. Explain yourself Teddy. This may not seem serious to you, but I have to respond to and address this. I can't have employees going to war with each other over paper clips and pencils."

"I understand."

"Do you? I like you Teddy, but you're going to have to get control over your anger. I noticed you seem particularly stressed lately. How are things at home?"

"Well, I'm still juggling work and taking care of my mother. I guess the stress of my responsibilities has built up and that's why I snapped when Bernadine came at me like that last week."

"Officially, I'm going to recommend you do two things. One, you will take a two-hour anger management course. Two, you will apologize to Bernadine. By the way, I'll be conferencing with her as well about how to avoid such unfruitful confrontation in the future."

"Okay," Teddy said graciously. He knew he could be in a lot more hot water had Bernadine or Gail pressed the issue. This was hardly his first office infraction. Admittedly, he was very familiar with the pecking order and disciplinary procedures once HR or the labor union got involved.

"Do I have your word this won't happen again?

"Yes," Teddy mumbled looking down at his hands he had unconsciously balled up into tensed fists. He hoped Gail was buying his promise to turn over a new leaf.

"Unofficially, I'm recommending you go see a doctor. Don't worry he's not a shrink. He has this B-12 supplement that does wonders for your mood. You'll be able to throw stress out the window. Trust me." Teddy was confused. He would be more amenable to seeing a therapist than a medical professional.

"B-12 is what you ask for as soon as you get there," Gail nodded and winked to imply that B-12 was code for something else.

What that something else was he had no clue. "Tell Dr. B. I sent you. He'll get you together lickety split," she snapped her fingers for emphasis. "Plus, it's all covered by our company's Blue Cross Blue Shield health insurance."

"Okay." For someone being reprimanded for verbally attacking his co-worker, Teddy was rather taciturn with Gail. His eyes glazed over as she whipped out the all too familiar documentation report. It was a standardized form that would have plenty of company in his ever-growing personnel record. He already knew the drill. One copy remained in Gail's files, one went to HR and the bottom carbon copy went to him. When Gail's metal file cabinet slammed shut, Teddy was relieved he was being issued yet another warning narrowly escaping suspension or termination. If an office could have a problem child, then he was it.

"This written reprimand will be in your personnel file for ninety days, but once you take the AM course and apologize to Bernadine, it will be removed. Does that sound like a workable plan Teddy?"

"Alright. I'll set aside some time later today to let you and Bernadine hash this whole mess out, you'll apologize, and we'll move on from here."

"Sounds fair," he said shaking Gail's hand glad to be given a chance to set things straight. Before he left, she handed him the business card of Dr. B.

"Keep this between me and you. Dr. B. is the plug," she almost whispered as she led him out of her office.

Teddy stared at the seemingly innocuous card. 'Dr. Benjamin O. Eagleston, D.O.', his office phone, address and a caduceus were embossed on the miniature placard. It wasn't fancy or flashy, but something about that wink and being "the plug" intrigued Teddy. Comfortably in the confines of his cubicle, he picked up the phone to make an appointment.

Chapter 11

Step Right Up

Teddy found a decent enough parking space in front of Dr. Eagleston's office. To his surprise, he was able to get a much-coveted late afternoon appointment within only three days. With Gail's blessing, he used his flex-time to leave work two hours early.

His check-in was rather routine. Naturally, he provided his health insurance information and the medical history form was a typical first visit checklist of medical ailments and present-day concerns. There was a small area asking for his known drug allergies. He was called back into a private room. That's when the odyssey began to look unlike any other healthcare service Teddy had ever received. He wasn't weighed or measured despite the fact a scale being one of the props present in Dr. Eagleston's patient care area. His temperature, blood pressure, and pulse weren't taken by the nurse. She had him sit on the examination table fully clothed. Teddy found it particularly odd that without assessing any of his vital signs, she had placed a syringe filled with an amber liquid on the medical console next to him. That must be the B-12 he thought. "The doctor will be right with you," the friendly freckle-faced nurse said as she slid the pocket door to his examination room closed.

Beads of perspiration had begun to form on Teddy's forehead and upper lip. He wasn't fond of needles AT ALL. Just looking at the cap on the syringe made him anxious. It never dawned on him that the B-12 treatments Gail personally endorsed would be given in the form of an injection. That was pertinent information she should have disclosed. Perhaps she assumed he already knew that. Maybe she knew that slight tidbit of information might dissuade him. In any case, he was too far in to turn back now.

He was jarred out of his angst about the ominous needle when there was a rapping on the door. The doctor slid the pocket door open and closed again deftly like he'd probably done hundreds of times a day. "Hello, I'm Dr. Ben Eagleston." He extended his hand to Teddy as he formally greeted him. "I know Eagleston is a mouthful, so you can just call me Dr. B. as many of my patients do. So, what brings you here today? How can I assist you?"

Where should he begin? The stress at home? The stress on the job? He opted to frankly tell Dr. B., "I was referred to you by my supervisor Gail Evans. She felt like I might benefit from your B-12 regimen."

"Ah, I see. You seek relief from fatigue or stress?"

"I guess a little of both," Teddy said softly. He felt like he was trying to give an adequate performance or explanation to be granted access to the special B-12 therapy Gail raved about to him.

Teddy's performance must have been stellar, because immediately Dr. B. pulled out his prescription pad. He added some chicken scratch to it and handed it to Teddy. "Take this to the dispensary down the hall. I've written you a particularly low dosage of dextroamphetamine, or D-Amp, to see how well you can tolerate it. Before you leave, make an appointment to return in a month. I'll evaluate your progress then."

"Okay." Teddy paused. His trepidation over the looming shot still had a powerful grip on him. "That's it? I don't have to get a shot?" asked Teddy nodding his head towards the syringe the nurse had left earlier.

"No, my friend. We just leave that with our new clients to see if they are junkies just trying to score drugs. You passed the test," Dr. Eagleston explained.

Teddy looked confused.

The doctor went over to the syringe, unscrewed the plastic cap and shot the contents in a continuous stream into the stainless-steel wash basin. "See just colored sugar water as harmless as Kool-Aid. I hope you aren't disappointed that I am not giving you a shot," Dr. B. said jokingly.

"Oh no, Doc. I hate needles. I'm quite relieved," Teddy told the doctor.

"Alright. Get that filled and I'll see you in a month," Dr. Eagleston instructed and vanished behind the pocket door presumably to another patient room.

Teddy hopped off the exam table. It might as well have been a comfy chair because no one had examined him. The good doctor didn't look in his eyes, ears, or nose. He didn't do that thing with the tongue depressor. He wasn't even given the opportunity to have a cold stethoscope pressed to his chest to verify a heartbeat. Dr. B. didn't check his reflexes. Sadly, his insurance would be billed the full amount for a new patient visit and consultation as if all of those had been properly conducted.

Teddy had never been to a physician who had his own onsite pharmacy. It was so convenient. He handed the attendant his hot-off-the-press prescription and she slid him three tiny envelopes of pills. It was smoother than any drugstore transaction he'd ever witnessed. A retail pharmacy would have typically taken at least twenty minutes to fill his prescription. That could only be the case if they had the requisite medication on hand. Dr. B. cut out the middle man, was adequately stocked to fulfill his need, and the service was billed directly to his insurance. How convenient.

When Teddy returned to his vehicle, he was amazed. His appointment was at 3:30 p.m.. The digital clock on his car's dashboard read 4:10 p.m.. He could get used to this in and out doctor arrangement. Hopefully, things would go just as smoothly on his next visit.

Chapter 12

The Good Doctor

"**P**apa, I need the check for the caterer and venue. You promised me last week you would take care of it," whined Penelope, Ben's youngest child and only daughter. She was seated across from him in her plush red terrycloth robe and giant pink hair curlers eating cottage cheese and peaches. She was on yet another fad diet trying to shed twenty pounds, a whole dress size, to fit into her bridal gown.

"Good morning to you too Daughter. How much is this going to cost me now my princess?" Ben was not too happy to keep hemorrhaging cash for Penelope's wedding, but it was tradition for the bride's family to foot the bill for their daughter's dream ceremony. Ben just wished in this instance, Penelope didn't dream so big. He also wasn't comfortable with her kitchen table attire. When he grew up, pajamas were a no-no at any meal.

Penelope rolled her eyes and let out a heavy sigh. "Papa, we've been over this a thousand times. The caterer is five and the venue is two."

"Dollars?" He asked playfully.

"Thousand Papa!"

"I'm just kidding you. I know the scale of this grand shindig. I apologize, I meant to say affair. Have your mother write out the checks for you. I have to get going. My first appointment is at 8:30 this morning."

"She already left for a spa day. Can't you just give me the checks?"

"I'm in a hurry. Plus, I don't have the checkbook. I make the money, but the Mrs. holds the purse. It is an arrangement that works for us. I'm sure you will do the same with Peter when you're finally hitched."

"Hitched Papa? I'm not a wagon being attached to a horse."

"Maybe you're the horse and he's the wagon?" he laughed. "I must go now. Have your mother pay the caterer and wedding hall. Have a nice day," he leaned down and kissed her on the forehead. He was gone before she could begin her protesting again.

Seated in the buttery soft leather seats of his Mercedes-Benz W126, Ben leaned back against the headrest. He didn't know how long he would keep up this financial facade. The real reason he couldn't simply hand his precious daughter seven thousand dollars was because he needed time to siphon the money from his business account. The truth was he was spending money ten times faster than he was making it. His income was a stellar six figures, yet his desires required a million-dollar budget. He was glad Zoe handled their household finances. She was a spendthrift who knew very well how to manage money, save it and invest it. He, on the other hand, wanted the finer things in life, all of them. What's more, he didn't want to wait for them. Inevitably, he would find a way to pay for and justify his extravagant expenses.

That's why he was creative in bringing in a constant flow of patients. He offered his trusted clients cash bonuses for new patient referrals. More patients meant more money for more toys like his customized boat, his vacation homes, and luxury cars. Somewhere along the way of doctoring he abandoned his oath to do no harm. His favorite prey were the sitting ducks or impoverished people around his office. They came equipped with government-backed insurance that paid him well. He kept them placated with synthetic feel-good meds dispensed from his cash cow onsite pharmacy. Most importantly, they were trusting of their good doctor. Rarely was he challenged on his unorthodox treatment plans. They got high, he got rich, it was a system that seemingly worked for all involved.

"Velma, can you call Fireproof to pick up the purged medical records for storage? We need to free up space in the file room," he directed his office manager.

"Sure boss," she greeted him with a toothy grin.

He was particular about his support staff. Anyone versed in proper standards of the primary healthcare industry would be a threat to his precarious scheme. He needed his clerical and nursing staff to be relatively green and unpolished. Hiring them fresh out of their training programs, they were pleased to have a job and especially grateful to be a part of the Eagleston Enterprise. They, like his patients, never challenged Dr. Ben. They never questioned why he spent less than ten minutes with his patients yet billed the office service as a full patient visit and consultation. They also believed the numerous identical B-12 treatments he prescribed were legit and sound medicine. Most importantly, they didn't see anything abnormal with the fact that truckloads of drugs were being dispensed out of the doctor's small private practice. He exploited their inexperience. They were unknowingly complicit in his complex set-up.

He did have one ethical boundary. He wouldn't allow any of his family or his staff's family to be treated in his office. He could have easily written Penelope a script for diet pills to melt away the pounds she was desperately trying to lose for her upcoming nuptials. Knowing his procedures weren't above board, he shielded his own flesh and blood from his subpar practices. In order to avoid ill feelings with his ancillary staff, he refused to accept them or their immediate family as patients.

"Who's the first patient?"

"Mr. Cortez Javier is in exam room five. I just love his name. He said you treated him when you were in medical school," Velma added looking over her bifocals at him.

"Which exam room?" He had heard her, but he was hoping he heard the patient's name incorrectly.

He gulped and then inhaled deeply and entered the tiny room

hoping it was anyone but CJ.

Chapter 13

Hoodwinked

"Good morning, Mr. Javier," said Ben despite one of his worst fears unfolding before him. Until this moment, Ben thought he was moving in the gay men's bath house underworld anonymously. Apparently, he was not. Seeing his secret lover in his office was never the intrusion he anticipated.

"You can drop the mister. After all we've known each other biblically so to speak," said Cortez batting his unusually long eyelashes at his now pale looking Sugar Daddy. Ben was one of the many sources of Cortez's livelihood. At the North High Street Sun bubble spa, he regularly entertained a veritable Who's Who of Columbus' powerful but closeted gay men. He had made this pop-up appointment because he was running low on supplies. . . the cash and drugs Ben supplied for services rendered. Fair exchange was no robbery. He just came to collect what he thought was rightfully his. His sugar from his daddy.

Ben hung his head in defeat. He had been intimate with Cortez, but he was explicit that their relationship needed to be and remain discrete. "What can I do for you CJ?"

"Look. Nobody out there knows we're acquainted. That's why I told them I was an old patient from your days as an intern. Clever, huh?"

"Yes. But why are you here? You are in my professional space. That is not part of our arrangement. What if Zoe had been here?" Ben despised being openly challenged on his own turf.

"Well, I'm pretty sure she would have mistaken me as a legitimate patient. Look, I came because I need money. I would lie and say it's for my ailing mother or something noble, but I just need it for all the wrong reasons," Cortez had grabbed Ben by the tie and planted a kiss directly under his chin. "You know what some of those wrong reasons are don't you?"

Ben cleared his throat and backed away from Cortez. "Look, this is highly inappropriate." Ben dug in his wallet, handed over the contents of his American eagle money clip, and asked "is this enough. It's all I have on me." The eagle's talons seeming useless no longer holding any cash in its clutches.

"Well, if you don't want news of just how inappropriate you've been with me, I suggest you bring me another fifteen hundred by tomorrow. I don't want to hear that 'I don't carry cash' excuse either. Please be a darling and write me a script for my cough," Cortez feigned a cough. CJ was not into the typical uppers, his drug of choice was painkillers.

Ben hurriedly filled out the script. "Don't fill it here. Do not come back here either," he said angrily through clenched teeth ripping the top page from his imprinted prescription pad. Ben, accustomed to being in control, didn't like being manipulated in this manner. But what other choice did he have? He couldn't risk being exposed as a same gender loving man. It would be scandalous and cost him his marriage, his reputation and his practice.   It was the mid-80s and gay men were wrongfully being scapegoated for the surge of AIDS. The very risk of contracting AIDS carried negative connotations. Being outted as a gay man could chase away his clientele. Cortez knew he could name his price for silence and Ben would pay it.

Chapter 14

The Spider, Bat & Owl

"Ahhh, oh my goodness! Teddy get down here now!" Thelma shrieked in a panic.

Teddy sprang into action. His feet barely touching the steps on his way downstairs to see what was the matter.

"Kill it! Kill it before it kills me!"

Teddy wasn't sure what "it" was, but he immediately understood it was his assigned duty to rectify the situation.

"It's a spider. The spider hissed at me. I swear I heard it hiss. I hope to God it's not poisonous. Please find it and kill it," said a breathless worried Thelma.

"It hissed? Only snakes hiss, Ma."

"It did. I'm scared. Please find it and make sure it is dead."

"What Ma? This little thing?" he quickly squished and held the destroyed arachnid up for Thelma to see on the end of a balled up paper towel.

"Get that thing outta my face. I can't stand spiders. Anything that don't pay a bill in this house or share my last name needs to go."

"Ma, you're being dramatic. Don't you think? Besides, you have on a shoe and walked past the broom to have me come all the way down here just to kill a teeny-weeny spider?"

"I don't care what you say. That thing is . . . was huge. It doesn't take much venom for them to kill you either."

"How do you know? You've never been bitten by a spider."

"No, but I was once attacked by a pack of wasps. They stung me in my face, my arms and my girls," she said pushing up her breasts to demonstrate.

"A pack? I think you mean swarm. Wasps, really? You're sure they weren't killer bees?"

"No. They were wasps. That's what they told me in the Emergency Room. They had to remove stingers from my boobs. It hurt like hell and I was embarrassed."

Teddy was trying not to laugh. He had heard this story a million times but it always became more deadly with each retelling. The stingers in his mom's chesticles tickled him the most every time.

"I just wanted to die. Luckily, the doctor told my mother not to let me sleep it off, but to get me to the ER right away. They said if I hadn't been treated with anti-venom my heart would have stopped," she clutched at her heart. Another part of Thelma's theatrics. "I would have died. I wouldn't be here now telling you this story. You wouldn't be here."

"And then what happened?" Teddy asked as if he didn't know the next bend in this all too familiar story.

"For the next two weeks, I had to take this medication that made me really groggy. It was bad timing because I was signed up for summer camp. It was a church camp. Even though I would be away from home, I would be with friends I already knew."

"That's nice. You weren't with strangers."

"I might as well have been. One night we had a sleepover in the barn. That was supposed to be a special night. We made a bonfire and roasted marshmallows. Mind you, this medication made me pass out like a light. I set up my pink polka dot sleeping bag pallet next to the window. It was August and all the hay had aggravated my allergies. My camp counselor thought being by the fresh night air might give me some relief."

"Makes sense," Teddy offered. Every time he heard this story, he was almost certain the counselor knew the possibility of what actually happened.

"After dinner, my counselor gave me my knockout pills. Then I had my moment with Skip. He was the boy I was crushing on at camp. It was puppy love for sure," Thelma tilted her head upwards and seemed to be genuinely transported back to this time of innocence. "He asked if he could have my phone number when we left Camp Hiawatha because he really liked me. See I know because I had slipped him a note. It read 'Do you like me?'. Underneath it, I drew three little boxes. One for Yes, one for Maybe and a very small one for No. I was trying to sway the vote so to speak."

"So, he said yes? But you let him get away and you ended up with The One Who Shall Not Be Named?"

"Let him slip away? I know he was only twelve, but that very night he failed me. Him and my best friend who signed up for camp with me. I woke up the next morning and not a soul was near me. Remember, I was by the window, but the other kids were flanked around me before going to bed. I wake up screaming, "Hey, where is everybody? Guys this isn't funny!"

"Where were they? Did they leave you there? Sounds like a sketchy camp if you ask me."

"Sketchy isn't even the word. There were two stories about why I was abandoned. The first told by best friend was that I was snoring so loudly by the time the rest of them were ready to bed down, they just retreated to the other side of the barn where it was quieter. The second told by Skip was that a bat had flown into the barn. Naturally, they opted to let the bat have his space in the window. However, they didn't want to wake me while they gathered safely on the bat-free side of the barn."

"Ah, that's messed up Ma. But last time I thought you said it was an owl and it woke you up with all the hooting."

"Owl, bat, or whatever. The point is Skip should have protected me. My best friend should have come to my rescue. They didn't and after that I became cynical. My motto is 'Trust no one'. My friend circle is a circle of one," Thelma drew an imaginary semi-circle around herself.

"I get it. But I'm almost sure it was an owl the last time you unfolded the camp story."

"Did you hear me, Son? The point is protection. Men are supposed to be providers and protectors. So as a man, your duty is to protect me, your mother. You're supposed to kill all my spiders. All of them!"

"Okay Ma. I got you. Spiders I don't mind. But a wise old owl once said, 'In a battle between you and a bat, you're on your own'.

Chapter 15

Led Astray

The crumbling parking lot of Eastgate Elementary School was brimming with cars. Some were forced to park on the grassy area leading towards the playground. Someone with better foresight, should have chosen a venue with adequate parking. Despite the minor inconvenience, people in fear of losing their homes were in attendance to learn of the fate of their neighborhood. Most had never been to an Eastgate Civic Association meeting. They came for answers to their burgeoning questions. Where was this new connector freeway going to go and when? Was it too late to reroute the project?

"Howdy Neighbor," said the lady already seated in one of the metal folding chairs arranged in the cafegymatorium.

"Hello?" replied Teddy. He wasn't sure if this woman actually knew him or if she was simply being polite.

"It's me. Miss Ouida from next door. I scared the hell outta you a few months ago and I haven't seen you since. I clean up good. Don't you think?"

"Well, I . . . " started Teddy. He was shocked to see Miss Ouida in a figure-flattering pantsuit rather than the baptism clothes his mother criticized. Her mostly raven black hair was gathered in a chignon at her nape. There were a few telltale gray hairs peeking out at him around her temples. He was speechless.

"You do remember me, right?"

"Yes, of course I do. I've never seen you so . . ." Teddy was grappling for the right words.

"Put together. I try," she volunteered a quick save.

"Yes. I've never seen you put together like this," Teddy said still in awe of Ouida's transformation. He began to wonder how old was she really? Maybe she would proposition him again. What did this café au lait version of Mrs. Robinson have in store for him? Seeing her in this light, he was more intrigued and not repulsed as he was by her on the fright night they shared earlier.

"Hmm. Hmm," his mother cleared her throat to bring Teddy's focus back to her.

"I'm sorry. Miss Ouida, this is my mother, Thelma Robinson. Mom this is Miss Ouida who's taking care of her brother, Mr. Bennett, next door."

"Pleased to meet you. I've seen you around. I just don't get out and about much," she told Ouida as she pointed to her cane.

"I totally understand. I'm sure I have seen you a time or two in the window. Now I can put a name with a face."

"Likewise."

"Ladies and gentlemen, if you'll be seated we can begin the meeting," said the Civic Association leader as he called the meeting to order. There was a quick reading of the previous meeting's minutes. Apparently, parliamentary procedure governed the flow of this gathering. Finally, they got to the matter at hand. The several city officials in attendance were formally introduced and each given a chance to take the floor to let the community know of their particular role in the implementation of the 670 project.

Skip Mulholland, Columbus City Council President was the first to speak. "Good evening. I'm glad you have come out to hear about our highway expansion plan. We are going to make every attempt to move forward with minimal effects on your homes and surroundings." He pulled his fingers through his sleek salt and pepper hair. He paused as if looking into some invisible camera. It was like he was lining up the right words to fire at these constituents demanding real forthright answers. "My colleague, Glenn Mansfield, is chairperson over the 670 Project. He can speak at length about the actual implementation plan," he said relieved to pass the baton of responsibility on to someone else. "Glenn, you take it way," Mulholland finessed his hair away from his brows again glad to no longer be in the hot seat.

"Oh well, Skip. You usually have a lot more to say," Glenn said looking flustered trying to get his notes in order. He had an unusually raspy and deep voice. It was one of authority but it definitely sounded like he had smoked cigarettes since the fourth grade.

"Folks, I'm excited about this new project. While unfortunately, some of you will be uprooted from your family homes and even some businesses will suffer, it is a necessary move in the direction for progress. The affected businesses and homeowners will be compensated. There will be noise barrier walls erected to protect the quiet enjoyment of those who remain. This particular stretch of highway will connect downtown Columbus to the Port Columbus International Airport. It will allow for ease of movement for travelers and city commuters alike. Mostly important is the economic development this will bring to the area. Simply put, it means jobs. Jobs created by the hotels, restaurants, and distribution facilities anticipated to be attracted to the 670 Corridor. I don't want to steal his thunder, so I'll let Solomon Steel tell you more about that," he said nodding at Solomon to have his turn at the podium. He too was glad to let someone else try to rationally explain why the governmental taking of their neighborhood was not only a good but great idea. It was a hard sell. Even for a seasoned politician. "Sol, you can give us more details."

Solomon Steel was a fair-skinned portly man with a perfectly shaped afro. He patted it gently before he began speaking. Just as he did, the mic gave out a shrill tone indicating interference. Perhaps it was a beacon of warning. He greeted the crowd and briefly introduced himself. He was giving a synopsis of his career to convince the crowd that he was more than qualified to serve as the community business liaison on this endeavor. "Like Councilman Mansfield alluded to earlier, this could generate jobs. Jobs that will generate opportunity and income for you and the economic opportunity will in turn create tax revenue for the City. Revenue that can be redirected into police and fire protection, libraries, sidewalk and road improvements," he was a veritable car salesman with a very slick approach. He flashed his porcelain veneers to the crowd, patted his meticulously maintained 'fro, and promised to be available for questions later.

Bray Brilmont, the area's State Representative, was also in attendance. When Mulholland returned to the podium he addressed him cordially. "Representative Brilmont, is there anything you would like to add?" Brilmont was a middle-aged man, brown-skinned, with a faint boyish moustache. He always held his head at a tilted angle as if everyone and everything was beneath him.

"No. You all have covered it all," he waved his hand like an old lady in church signifying her approval of what the preacher just said. It was the 'Go 'head preacher preach' gesture. This decision to remain seated and silent was strategic. If he couldn't be quoted, then consequently he couldn't be challenged at election time. The last thing he needed was any of these people saying he promised they wouldn't lose their homes or businesses to the I-670 project. All told, it was a classic example of when elected leadership fails the community at large.

It was an hour after the beginning of the meeting before the Eastgate residents were finally able to address the panel of politicians and officials. The bad thing about politicians is that they talked more than they listened. When their constituents needed them the most to stand up and represent, was usually the time they chose to sit down in silence just like Brilmont.

Once the floor was open for public commentary, Ouida surprisingly went to the podium to speak first. She wanted to know why the Eastgate community was in the path of the freeway at all.   If a route from downtown Columbus to the airport was the desired result, then this was not the most direct way to go about it.   Her direct question was "if the shortest distance between point A and point B is a straight line like we were taught in geometry, then why is the project's current design plan meandering through and busting up the predominantly poor, Black neighborhoods of Eastgate and Shepard?" Not one man on the ad hoc panel had a succinct and coherent answer to this woman's inquiry. She had done her homework and they had expected her, along with her neighbors, to accept their impending freeway development announcement without challenge.

"Teddy. Take me up there. I have something to say," demanded Thelma. He obeyed and escorted his mother up front to address the panel.

"When I was a little girl, I grew up in a part of the city called Flytown. It doesn't exist anymore because it was leveled in the name of improving our fine city. I don't have a family home to return to on holidays like Thanksgiving unless I want to be mowed down by highway traffic. I am haunted to this day of that unexpected uprooting. I'm tired of being called upon to sacrifice my happy home for the so-called greater good. Black people like me can't seem to catch a break. As members of the African diaspora, we were stolen from a faraway land. We still can't seem to gain a good foothold in this foreign land. Growing up, I never had much. My parents did the best they could to give us a decent place to live, a home, only to have it knocked down as rubbish. I tried to do the best for my son here," she pointed to Teddy to emphasize he was the impetus for her struggle to survive and succeed. "My house might not measure up as a mansion, but it's all I have to call home. I can't let you take what's rightfully mine away from me. I think I speak for everyone here who is tired of being displaced, misplaced and replaced. We belong here. We're resolved to stay!" The crowd applauded loudly. Only time would tell which families would or would not remain steadfast and unmovable.

Chapter 16

The Cookie Begins to Crumble

Teddy was headed into the store for tomato paste. On Saturday, he had mistakenly bought tomato sauce. Thelma insisted she needed it for her Monday night meatloaf. So, he was duty bound to correct his market mistake. He was surprised and happy to see Angela outside when he pulled into the parking lot.

"Hey Pretty Lady, you on break?" Teddy asked.

"No. I might be out of a job. I just came out here to get some fresh air," Angela replied. "They just told us the store is closing. This one and the one at Parsons and Livingston. With the new freeway proposal, Corporate agreed to a land swap with the City and they're planning to build a new location further south. What's worse is we're being offered jobs at the new store, but I can't walk there like I do now. I barely make enough money to take care of me and my baby girl. I can't afford a car. I could take the bus, but the extra travel time means more money for full-time instead of part-time childcare. It's just a bit overwhelming."

"Oh. I see. Things will work out for you. I'm sure. I could take you to work, but that would require you giving me those golden digits," he offered slyly.

"Nice try. You know I couldn't do that," she gave him a light punch in his arm.

"Can't do what? Give me your number or grant me the honor and privilege to carry you to work?"

"Both."

"Ouch. Well don't say I didn't offer."

"Thanks, I really do appreciate the gesture."

"It's not a gesture. I really wouldn't mind."

"I could use a lift home. I've got to lug a big case of diapers home."

"Say no more. When do you get off?"

"As soon as I buy the diapers. I'm not officially on the clock. I just came in for the store meeting. I can't believe they drug us in here to break bad news like this on a Monday."

"Monday is as fitting as any other day," he observed aloud.

"You're probably right."

"I know I'm right."

Teddy wasn't exactly sure what he expected to see when he pulled up to Angela's crib. It left a lot to be desired. To guard the less than luscious estate was a German Shepherd. He barked the instant Teddy got there.

"Don't worry about Killer. He doesn't bite."

"You say that, but does he know it?"

"Thanks for the ride, Teddy."

"No problem. Anytime you need a ride you just let me know. Seriously. No strings attached."

"Okay." She got out and made her way to the remnants of a screen door. Maybe it and the dog had engaged in a disagreement. Teddy didn't want any confrontation with the chained dog, especially one named Killer, so he waited in his car until he saw that Angela was safely inside. He then headed home for some of his mother's can-it-get-any-drier meatloaf. His Monday night mainstay.

* * *

"Settle down gentlemen. I have great news to share with you. The freeway development is moving forward, but Reclamation Church will be left fully intact. Apparently, the City chose a route that will allow several landmark churches to narrowly escape the path of the construction. Trinity Baptist, Shiloh Baptist and of course our edifice will only abut the highway. We've been informed that we will be minimally affected. The City will provide traffic cops to allow easy access to and egress from our church property during the nearby project construction.

"So, is this a separation of Church and State thing?" asked Deacon Sideris.

"Not in a literal sense. Some churches in the Leonard Avenue area will still be consumed by the project. But they were already boarded up properties. According to Daniel Vogel, our legal counsel, the government can swoop in and take church property that has relatively no or little value. That usually means dilapidated and neglected buildings are prime for taking by Eminent Domain. One tenth of the land we occupy is worth more than a million dollars. As it stands, we're far exceeding the criteria to fall to this 670 Project."

"I think this calls for a celebration," said Metropolitan.

"Hmm hmm," Vogel said clearing his throat and rising to greet the Church Council members. "There's the issue of my fee. It must be voted upon by a majority here before it can be paid".

"Damn lawyers always chasing the almighty dollar," mumbled Petrov Babalos to the men closest to him. He had been embroiled in a nasty divorce a few years earlier. His wife had hired the best representation. Her lawyer easily found assets he had been trying to hide for years. His disdain for attorneys and domestic court judges was deeply rooted in bitterness.

"All in favor of reimbursing Mr. Vogel for his fee of," Metropolitan hesitated while he donned his readers to find the dollar figure on the invoice Vogel had handed him moments earlier. "Twenty-five thousand dollars?" he half said and half questioned as he looked at Vogel to confirm if the amount was correct.

Vogel nodded and buttoned his perfectly tailored Ralph Lauren suit jacket as if he was proud and pleased with himself. After all, he had fulfilled his obligation to be the Church's Superman to fly in, swoop down, and save the day.

"Twenty-five? Thousand? Dollars? That's highway robbery! Why exactly are we being charged so much? Can we get a breakdown of that fee? I paid that much for my last divorce and we were embroiled in court for eighteen months. You didn't even have to litigate this matter. I want more answers," Babalos demanded.

"Well, I can understand your concern, but I feel this is a small price to pay to save our beloved church house," the Metropolitan felt obliged to sway the Church Council vote because Vogel had been instrumental in smoothing out several legal wrinkles for him personally in the past. Collecting this fee from Reclamation was actually a repayment padded intentionally for the pro bono work Vogel had done to save his bacon in the past. "All in favor of honoring this invoice for services rendered say 'aye'." All of the council members voted to approve paying the attorney fees except Babalos who remained silent and crossed his arms to signify his discontent.

"As I was saying earlier, I think this calls for a celebration," Metropolitan said loudly towards the kitchen. As if on cue, Growlin rolled out a serving cart. It carried a fresh bottle of ouzo and a stack of disposable communion wine cups. There was also a tray of feta and spinach pinwheel sandwiches from the nearby Kroger deli. The men were also blessed with leftover mints and nuts from the last fellowship hall gathering. It would be just enough to absorb the alcohol and they could leave Reclamation tipsy rather than totally inebriated.

"To Reclamation standing tall forever," Metropolitan declared raising his cup in a toast. "Salud!"

"Salud!" the men repeated in unison. Now that the church was no longer in danger of being bulldozed, the council and congregation could return to church business as usual mode.

Chapter 17

Didn't See That Coming

Tensions were building at work. It was nearing the fiscal year end. Everyone was nervous about the prospect of whether or not they would have a job in a few months. Empty posts were not being back-filled. Most of middle management had taken early retirement buyouts or left altogether. Gail was now over the lingering remnants of two units that were once comprised of fifty administrative staff and four supervisors and assistant supervisors. The attrition due to retiring workers or lateral promotions meant those remaining in Teddy's department were highly stressed and overworked.

Gail, like most, was experiencing turmoil on the home front as well. Unfortunately, she was bringing her outside drama to work with her. Interpersonal conflicts that inevitably arose among her employees were allowed to fester. Several union grievances were brought against her calling out her lack of leadership and unfair treatment. She was running a sinking ship as a very absent-minded captain. Although her underlings weren't privy to her B-12 therapy, they felt like she was definitely on something.

"Teddy, can I please see you in my office?" Gail asked.

"Sure Gail. What is up?" he said as he closed the door to her office. Her tone was serious. He noticed her eyes were bloodshot. He couldn't be certain, but he thought he detected alcohol on her breath. He dismissed the notion because he didn't think she would jeopardize her good government job by doing such a thing.

"I'm about to take a p-p-protracted personal leave of absence," she said both stammering and slurring her words.

"Oh. Is this the beginning of the end? You can be honest with me," Teddy knew she was sauced now. If he was being let go sooner rather than later, then he wanted to know. He was ready to bite the bullet and take the bad news like a man.

"No. Not at all. In fact, everyone under my level has job security. But here's the deal," she tried to look Teddy in the eye but kept shaking her head and blinking as if she were seeing double.

"Deal?"

"In my absence, you'll be acting supervisor. Isn't that great?" she tried to exhibit joy for Teddy, but pills and alcohol were coloring her thoughts, words, and subsequently her emotions.

"But why me? I don't have any supervisory experience," he wondered out loud.

"Look. That's exactly what I said," she half-pointed at him and pulled out an icy blue pint-sized bottle of Bombay Sapphire gin and poured some in her coffee cup. Why did Americans import products to satisfy their guilty pleasures? He shook his head in disbelief. Freedom of choice was a wonderful privilege. He personally chose Hennessy or Wild Turkey when he did imbibe. The domestic brand of course being the most budget friendly.

"Shh!", she shushed him even though he was not talking. "I think they picked you simply because you are a man. It's like they think that hangy downy thing between your little skinny frail legs makes you a natural-born leader. As a friend, I'm sorry to insult you Teddy, but you know you have pencil legs. But that's beside the point. You'll be paid my salary until I return. When I do, you're next in line for a supervisory position. Isn't that great? Whoop! Whoop! Hurray for you!" she said raising her mug in a mocking celebratory gesture.

"Look Gail, I'm not exactly sure what you're going through right now. I do know you're in no state to drive yourself home. As your friend who cares, please let me drive you home."

"Wow! You can't wait to get rid of me."

"Nothing of the sort. I just don't want this momentary lapse in judgment to cost you your job. You're my boss, but you're also my friend. You've looked out for me a time or two."

"You're damn right I have!" she half slurred and half shouted having lost her perception of volume control after a few too many.

He left momentarily to grab a cup of black coffee. He would need to sober Gail up first. At least to a point that he could help her safely walk through the breezeway and not stumble to the parking garage.

He pulled the blinds down in her office and let her sleep it off for a bit. When she had rested, he managed to get her relatively unscathed into her vehicle. He drove her home. He'd been to her home several times for barbecues, birthday celebrations, or just to pick up or drop off urgent paperwork. He had driven with the windows down and the fresh air seemed to help Gail's complexion return to normal and gradually lift her out of her inebriated stupor.

He walked in with her. The house was eerily quiet. He wanted to ask about the realty sign on her front lawn, but figured this wasn't a good time to pry.

"I'll call myself a cab. You get some rest. I'll make sure the department doesn't fall apart without you," Teddy felt awkward being Gail's questionable replacement.

"Thanks Teddy," Gail said.

On the way home, Teddy thought about Gail's misgivings about his ability to lead the troops while she was gone. While he often felt like he could do just as good of a job as Gail, his confidence didn't lie solely on being a man. Other than supervisory experience, he had the same credentials as she did. He looked down at his legs. He didn't think that they resembled number two pencils at all. He chuckled because he knew drunk minds speak sober thoughts. Perhaps there were worst things for Gail to say or think about him.

Chapter 18

Drunken Brawl

"**Y**ou know what makes me madder than hell?" Teddy leaned in as if he was going to reveal a deep secret to his new found friend, Keith, Papa Jack's bartender.

"Nah Man. What?" answering Teddy's question with a question.

"They only promoted me to do the dirty work my lady boss couldn't. The higher-ups wanted me to choose who to keep on the team and who to cut loose. It just seemed so arbitrary. In under a month, I dismissed four people I had worked with for years. People I consider more than just colleagues, but friends. Well, all except that old bitty Bernadine. It was kinda fun firing her. I finally passed the last lick between us. She was always complaining and making my work life a parallel hell. I can't be sure, but I think she had her son vandalize my car. For an older lady, her reaction was extremely immature."

"Yeah Man. That's messed up. But when you push somebody over the edge, you can't be surprised by their over-the-top reaction," Keith shook his head and wiped down the area next to Teddy for an approaching customer.

"Yeah. No doubt," he barely said before being rudely interrupted by a guy who was standing dangerously close behind him.

"You the jerk that's been messin' over my woman?" the angry man nudged Teddy on his shoulder. Judging by his snorts and flared nostrils, he was more than ready to pick a fight.

"Man keep your hands off of me! Who are you? What woman? Can't you see I'm here alone . . . minding my business? I suggest you do the same," he retorted.

"That's where you're wrong. Ranessa is my business. She came home empty-handed after you tied up her time a while back and then stiffed her for the night. You ready to settle up punk?"

"I ain't no punk. I ain't paying you or your girl nothing. You got me bent," Teddy stood up and squarely met the heated gaze of his challenger.

"Let's go!" Ranessa's business manager snarled at Teddy while pounding his left fist into his right hand to punctuate his violent demand.

"Yo, yo, yo! Hold up! Take that mess outside. Derrick, I see you're upset, but I can't have y'all jeopardizing my liquor license. The City's already yanked our Sunday open privileges. Out! Both of you!"

"So, it's like that Man? Don't worry about me. I've been put out of much better. Trust and believe me," Teddy said with white hot indignation. He paid his tab throwing two twenties on the bar towards Keith. He had knocked back several shots and beers trying to drown his workplace sorrows. His inebriation had emboldened him. His intention was to leave the bar. However, Ranessa's pimp was ready to follow through with his earlier threat to settle the score with bodily harm if necessary.

Blam! Was the sound that reconnected Teddy with some modicum of sobriety. Derrick, a stocky muscle-bound brute, had body slammed Teddy into his car door. It was another sneak attack from behind.

"You shouldn't have done that," declared Teddy. He then upper cut and drop kicked his attacker.

"Man. Okay. Okay. I was just kidding. No harm. No foul. I don't want no problems," backing away and resorting to a much more passive tone.

"Oh, so now you don't want these problems? Really?" Teddy asked facetiously as he kicked his fallen opponent in his bloated stomach.

"Ow Man. You win," Derrick grimaced in pain as he admitted

defeat. "We good. Call us even," he tried pleading with Teddy to stop as he tried in vain to roll away from him on the uneven sidewalk.

"Why (kick) couldn't (kick) you (kick) just (kick) leave (kick) me (kick) alone?!" Teddy raged. It was not the outcome Derrick expected. Quickly, the merciless predator had turned into the humbled and pitiful prey.

Silence. Then sirens. The cops had arrived. Moments later an ambulance came to rescue the bloody and bruised Derrick.

"You're under arrest for assault and battery," said the taller cop as he handcuffed Teddy and simultaneously began to inform him of his Miranda rights.

"Who me? I'm the victim here! He was trying to shake me down for money," Teddy didn't want to divulge the nature of the transaction that prompted their interaction. He knew exposing Derrick as a pimp would cast him in the role of one soliciting a prostitute. He definitely didn't want the authorities believing that about him. "He attacked me. I was simply defending myself," Teddy protested.

"Forgive me if it doesn't look that way. You can try selling that story to the judge. I don't see a scratch or scrape on you. The other guy looks like he's been through a meat grinder. Now duck!" the officer barked loudly as he pushed Teddy into the backseat of his cruiser.

Chapter 19

So You Think You're Better?

"**M**r. Robinson, is it?" asked the drug counselor peering over water puddle-looking black-rimmed bifocals at Teddy.

"Yeah, who are you?" Teddy was curt with his new adversary. Teddy had been placed in a straitjacket after he head-butted another patient in group therapy. He couldn't recall exactly what had prompted the attack. The target's head was unforgiving and Teddy had essentially knocked himself silly upon impact. Staff immediately restrained him and now he was in this ring of the circus with yet another clown.

"I'm Lionel Stone your new therapist. We typically don't provide individual counseling until you're further along nearing the end of the treatment program. However, due to your violent outburst earlier today, we feel the need to engage with you in intense individual therapy. Please do not mistake the fact that you've graduated to this point as an indication of positive progress."

"No offense Doc, but I've got a pounding headache. Can you please explain to me what's going on? What are you saying? You're talking in riddles and circles. Clearly, I can't hurt you," Teddy tried feebly to lift his arms to emphasize his point. "What are you trying to tell me? I failed your little rinky dink rehab program? I'll tell you like I've told my boss, my attorney, the prosecutor and the ring leader ass clown in the group session, 'I'M FINE. I DON'T NEED HELP!'"

"Let's examine that statement. I'll ignore the fact that you being court-mandated to complete our rehabilitation assessment and program think that I am going to tolerate your insolence. I will not! Do not raise your voice at me again Mr. Robinson!"

Teddy looked down hopelessly and helplessly at the securements crossing his midsection beginning to accept this as just another consequence of his misguided actions and bad decisions.

"Look in this mirror Mr. Robinson. Granted, looks can be deceiving, but between me and yourself who seems on face value to be in need of help?"

"Me," mumbled Teddy. It was a humbling moment. Seeing the reflection of his unshaven face and matted 'fro was indeed off putting. He didn't like this lesser version of himself one bit. He looked like he'd fought life and life definitely had won.

"My colleague tells me you absolutely refuse to participate in the group counseling sessions. You openly scoff at the other patients. Is that true?"

"Yes. I'm not no drunk or meth head. I may overindulge a bit, but my meds are prescribed by my doctor for a legitimate health condition."

"Your doctor gave you these pills, right?"

"Yes."

"Did his signing off on providing you access to a legal substance give you the desired outcome? Were the side effects supposed to be nearly losing your job, landing in jail and now rehab?"

"No."

"I posit the drunks you look down in group aren't much different from you. The government has sanctioned the use of alcohol. Yet the same government accepts no responsibility for the detrimental use of the alcohol that is freely supplied on nearly every street corner in America. They visit a liquor store be it clean or dirty. They drink to excess until their everyday lives enter into a downward spiral that has led them here. Are you following me?"

Teddy nodded. His repulsive reflection was still bothering him.

"You on the other hand, take your script to a well-regulated hopefully clean blue ribbon, A-one drug store, a legal apothecary, and acquire a substance that has the same ability to wreak havoc on your life. The optics may be different but the outcome is the same. You're addicted Teddy. Don't you get it?"

"I'm not like them. I'm different."

"Birds of a feather flock together. Contrary to what you deduce, you belong here. As they say on The *Spaceship Odyssey* 'you have found your people'. What was your drug of choice on the outside Teddy?"

"Amphetamines."

"Are you serious right now? Do you even know the history of the abuse of amphetamines?"

"What? Doc you're speaking in riddles again. Please make it plain."

"You've heard of Adolph Hitler and the Third Reich?"

"Of course, I have. What does Hitler and Nazism have to do with me other than this set-up being like a concentration camp?"

"That is where you are wrong my friend. Hitler would dose his soldiers with amphetamines so they could continually march into enemy territory without the benefit of sleep. It gave them the ability to succeed with their Blitzkrieg tactics. Haven't you been using, or shall I say more accurately abusing this legal drug, to reap an illicit benefit?"

"I ain't no damn Nazi!"

"I never said you were. I just want you to see you're in good company with other folks who find themselves struggling with an unhealthy addiction to a substance they legally have access to. Forty percent of the drugs abused by Americans were prescribed by their physician. While you might be different Mr. Robinson, you're definitely not better. Thanks to your diversion program, you, like them, have landed on the same heap. Remember that."

"I still don't think I should be lumped in the same category."

"What category is that Snap Wilson?" Dr. Stone trying desperately to connect civilly with a hostile Teddy.

"Ah, the Falcon. How do you know about my avian alter ego?" Teddy asked slyly raising an eyebrow. Maybe relaying your fanciful belief that you're the embodiment of a fictional comic book character to a therapist wasn't such a good idea. Especially while you are freshly suited up in a straitjacket.

"Call it a lucky educated guess. Most people don't seek help until they have reached rock bottom and find themselves looking up. Welcome to Rock Bottom Teddy. We here at Phoenix Rising hope you'll love the meager accommodations and enjoy your stay," Dr. Stone said facetiously.

Teddy was growing more irritated by Dr. Stone. He was sick of doctors and medical professionals in general. He sat quietly with no response to rebuff his accurate assessment.

"The sooner you realize you've landed yourself squarely in the same mess as our other clients, then your road to recovery can truly begin."

"Okay. I get it. So, what do I have to do here exactly?"

"First, let's explore why you think you use. Is there a particular reason? Was it recreational and then over time it became a problem. Are you mimicking behavior modeled by your parents? Addiction fills a void. Help me see your full picture."

"I was pretty stressed and having issues with my temper at work. My supervisor recommended this quack of a doctor who turned me onto the stuff. I regret ever taking that advice," he reflected on the role Gail and Dr. Eagleston played in leading him to the shore of this newfound doom.

"Were your parents addicts?"

"What do my parents have to do with me popping pills every now and again? My mother is sober as a judge, but my father is a drunk to hear her tell it."

"You didn't grow up with your father in the home?"

"No. The stories my mother tell me make him out to be a Boogie Man on steroids in need of an exorcism. He got in touch with me a while back after he remarried and started going to church. He went to some VIP Sweat Lodge with Utah Jazz's Karl Malone. Afterwards, he came to me to atone for walking out on me and my mother. All of the heat must have taken him to a hallucinogenic level, because he just wanted to wipe the slate clean and be pals again. Just chalk up my childhood abandonment as a misunderstanding so we could become bosom buddies. He wanted my unconditional personal forgiveness for a questionably ambiguous accountability. He apologized for not being there for me as a kid. Forget about never tossing, kicking or throwing a ball around with me. Forget about not showing me how to shave, ride a bike, tie a tie or treat a lady. Forget about unfairly thrusting me into the role of man of the house at age five. I told him he could shove his apology up his ass and I've never heard or seen him again. I guess it made him feel better about himself. It just made me feel like the awkward fatherless kid with more questions than answers. It was like he had pushed me off a cliff and then wanted to be applauded as the hero who came to my rescue after I somehow managed to survive the deadly fall. I'm sorry to say I don't know my father well. Doc, do you think addiction is in my genes? Like I can't escape what is in my DNA?"

"There are documented studies saying yes, but in my opinion, addiction speaks to the human condition. We all have a need or void and sometimes we fill that emptiness with harmful things like drugs, food, alcohol, compulsive shopping, or gambling."

"My mom smokes and suffers from pica."

"See that's what I mean. You had a primary influence modeling addictive behavior to you as a child. The two of you may have had different reasons and different substances, but the use to excess is the creation of a problem."

"Oh. I see," said Teddy as if he was indeed processing the therapist's information.

"I think we have covered enough today. Is it safe to assume you have calmed down? I can have those restraints removed if you promise to behave."

"I promise. Scout's honor. Sorry, I can't cross my heart or give you a salute," Teddy tried lifting his elbows to emphasize his immobilization predicament.

Dr. Stone pressed an intercom button on his phone. "Nurse, can you call staff to have Mr. Robinson returned to his room? I'm issuing an order to remove his present restrictions as long as there are no further incidents," he looked distinctly at Teddy as he pronounced the last phrase. His look let Teddy know that if there was one misstep, he'd be back in the straitjacket like a clipped wing bird. Something neither of them wanted.

Chapter 20

Double Trouble: Uninvited Wedding Guests

Penelope Eagleston's transition from being a daddy's girl to a blushing bride went off without a hitch. She and Peter were wed in a short church ceremony at Reclamation Greek Orthodox Basilica.

Besides the family members who had traveled from near and far, there were several colleagues of Ben and Zoe present. The opulent affair had been prepared for three hundred guests and it seemed like every one invited showed up. Unfortunately, a few stragglers came who were not invited by the bride nor the groom. They were bold and presumptuous to join the reception as "plus ones". Weddings don't typically have bouncers, so they slipped in quite easily among the crowd.

The first interloper was Heather Groetzky, an old girlfriend of Ben's from Harrisburg, Pennsylvania. Ben was shocked to see her. He knew he hadn't included her on any guest list. They hadn't spoken since his second year of undergrad.

"Why Ben Darling, it is such a pleasure to see you again after all these years. What has it been about thirty or so?" she asked. She also reached up to run her fingers through the grey hairs which framed Ben's face right at the temples of his hairline.

"Yes. I guess so," he said firmly removing her gnarly fingers from his face. He hoped Zoe wasn't around to witness this exchange. He hadn't seen Heather in years. Why had she traveled all the way to Ohio on this day of all days? His primary focus was to get through Penelope's day with as little drama as possible.

"Imagine my surprise when I read Penelope's wedding announcement in the socialite section of the *Harrisburg Gazette*. I hope you don't mind. I wouldn't miss this for the world. I could have been her mother. As I recall, you were dead set against having children when we were together. What happened?"

"Heather, I don't want to be an ungracious host, but I'd rather not discuss our days of yesteryear and what you might think could or should have been between us. Excuse me. It's time for the father-daughter dance. Help yourself to some refreshments," he said and hurried over to what he hoped would be a safe haven at Penelope's side.

"Mother, I can get it," complained Penelope trying to bustle her gown so she could dance freely without damaging her train.

"Well at least let me hold your bouquet," Zoe said fussing over her baby turned bride.

The DJ began to play. Ben was so proud of Penelope as she crossed this majestic threshold of womanhood. Hopefully motherhood would soon follow. His little girl was all grown up now.

"Daddy, I think I'm about to be sick," Penelope walk-limped as fast as she could to the ladies' room. Zoe chased after her.

"Not what you expected, huh? Doc?" said Cortez.

"I . . . uh, what? What are you doing here?"

"Don't you recognize me? I'm the help," said Cortez. He was dressed in the same attire as the other servers. He had maneuvered his way into the festivities as wait staff. It was a clever move.

"What are you doing here?" With the hubbub of the wedding, Ben was not able to meet up with CJ like he usually did. He was finding it harder to juggle his personal and professional finances to funnel money to his playboy.

"I've come to collect what's mine. You should know by now that you cannot avoid me," he whispered. CJ stood shoulder to shoulder with Ben. He was leaning in as if to listen for instructions to convince the others he was a legitimate server and not an extorting lover. "Our agreement is that you keep me in the lifestyle for which I am now accustomed. It's time to pay up for services rendered and more importantly my silence."

"Meet me outside in ten minutes," Ben ordered through clenched teeth. He couldn't afford to have CJ embarrass him in front of all his friends and family. It would ruin his beloved daughter's most special day.

"Okay. I love it when you're demanding," CJ smiled and winked at Ben.

Ben was mortified. What if someone had seen CJ openly flirting with him? He moved away from him quickly hoping no one was privy to the true nature of their relationship.

"Zoe. Zoe what's wrong with Penelope?" he stood and shouted through the door to the ladies' restroom.

"Ben, I think she is just exhausted. Today has been a lot of excitement for all of us," Zoe explained. If Zoe got wind of CJ and Heather slithering their way into the reception, he would probably end up being physically ill too.

"I'm going to send in some ginger ale. You're sure she's alright?" He thought it ironic that as a classically trained physician, in a pinch he was reduced to handing out an old home remedy. Not only was it basic, but he did so without bilking an insurance company for it. Focus Benjamin. This is family for goodness' sake. His flim-flam medical menacing could resume on Monday morning.

"Yes. We'll be out in a bit," Zoe reassured him as she continued playing her dual roles of concerned mama bird and mother of the bride.

"I'll be right here," he lied. He told a waitress to take Penelope some ginger ale and water before dipping out to the parking lot to meet CJ.

"What is the matter with you coming here like this? Around

my family?" Ben asked sternly. He didn't want to attract any attention to them.

"Ay, Papí. I need you. I need you to pay my rent, my car note, and my taxes," CJ said batting his eyelashes.

"Taxes? What you do isn't even legal to be taxed."

"I know. I just like seeing you all riled up. So just write me a check and I'll go."

"A check? Are you crazy? There's no way I am going to leave a paper trail with you! Look! Meet me Monday at our spot. I'll have your money then. Will five thousand suffice?"

"For now."

"I will bring your favorite . . . cash."

Chapter 21

Time To Pay Up

Ben was anxious to meet with CJ. He wanted to pay up and be done dealing with him. Somehow, he knew their meeting would involve more than the expected cash transaction.

"Hi Bob," the Sun Bubble attendant greeted him from behind the avocado colored formica counter. Bob was his alias at the spa. He made every effort to keep this part of his life a secret. He didn't think of himself as gay. While he was a happily married man, he simply enjoyed the company of a man also. It wasn't love only lust. To him, that justified his duality.

"Hello. Is Dan here?" 'Dan' was CJ's handle at the private bath house. He knew CJ was already inside because his BMW was parked near the rear entrance. "Room 8?"

"You guessed it," said the attendant. He quickly returned to reading the *Dispatch*. This had to be the easiest gig in town. Greet the customers, collect their money, and hand out towels. It was a starving artist's or college student's dream job. To make ends meet, they could earn extra money for special favors if they chose. The hot tub maintenance was contracted to an outside service provider. Hands down, it was an easy job.

The spa decor left much to be desired. Every door was numbered and named after a tropical animal. Ben and CJ's spot was the Parrot Room. It was just easier to call it what it was. . . Room Eight.

Ben slipped into the dimly lit rendezvous point. He closed the door behind him.

"Well, hello. I'm glad you came. I didn't want to have to chase you down again."

"That won't be necessary," said Ben slipping a banded stack of fifty one hundred dollar bills into CJ's jacket pocket.

"Thank you Papí," CJ said sarcastically air kissing him with puckered duck lips. "Come come. It feels great in here."

Ben disrobed down to black swim trunks and then eased into the steamy hot tub.

"Why are you over there? I don't bite," said CJ as he seductively winked at Ben to entice him to come closer.

"I think we need to go over the rules of engagement. I cannot have you inserting yourself in my life. At my practice? At my daughter's wedding? That's totally not a part of our deal."

"I know. I'm sorry. I won't do it again. I promise."

It sounded like a hollow promise to Ben. He wanted to take CJ at his word. He couldn't afford to have Zoe find out about his double life.

"You brought the sugar, but are you ready for some candy Daddy?" CJ asked seductively.

Ben didn't answer. He wished he had just paid CJ and left. But here he was doing the dance with him again.

"Ahhh," was the sigh Ben released as CJ began to work his steamy magic under the bubbling water.

* * *

"Hello," said Zoe.

"Good morning Mrs. Eagleston. This is Clark Redmond from Black Crow Savings & Loan."

"Okay. How can I help you?" She couldn't imagine why the bank would be calling her so early on a Monday morning. She had shifted some money around to cover the last-minute outlays they had made for Penelope's wedding. Surely, they had adequate funds to cover the outstanding checks.

"I wanted to inform you that a large cash withdrawal was made. I believe you set this account up with fraud alerts. This is just a courtesy call to hold up our end of the bargain. If you believe this is fraudulent activity, then I can transfer you to our Fraud Department and they can further assist you."

"No. That won't be necessary." She hung up the phone. She knew she had given Penelope a few blank checks while the wedding plans were coming together. Deep down she knew Penelope wouldn't make such a large withdrawal. Right? Would she? Ben didn't typically use their personal account for such large sums either. She needed to ask both of them before launching a formal investigation with the bank's Fraud Department. It would take two quick phone calls.

* * *

"Penelope Love. Is there something you need to tell me?" Zoe asked hoping her daughter had simply forgotten to tell her about a rather large bank transaction due to the hubbub of the wedding.

"My gosh Mom I can't keep anything from you. How did you know? Was it because I got sick at the reception?"

"No. Wait. What are you talking about exactly?"

"I'm talking about you being a grandmother in six and half or seven months. We'll have a more specific due date after my ultrasound."

"What?! You're pregnant? Congratulations! I can't believe this. No wonder you couldn't lose those last ten pounds before the wedding."

"You're not upset?"

"Why would I be? I think you and Peter will be the perfect parents to my perfect grandchild. So, you reversed the marriage and carriage by a few months. No harm. No foul. Does your father know? I'm sure he could recommend a great ob-gyn."

"No. I haven't told him yet.   Thanks for offering a referral, but I'm pretty happy with my present doctor. Besides, Dad is so hands off about doctoring on me. He still thinks of me as his little princess. Remember when I was a developing teenager, he almost had a coronary when you told him I started my period. I'll figure out a way to break the news to him gently."

"Please don't be blindsided if Metropolitan won't allow the baby's christening. You know how strict the orthodox faith is about such matters. It's their rules Honey . . . not mine.

"I'm not worried about that. I just want to focus on having a healthy baby."

"That's the spirit. Positive vibes only," Zoe said trying to reassure her baby who was having a baby everything would be alright. Deep down she knew for the right price, church leadership would allow Barnum & Bailey to rent out the sanctuary for their grand circus. She had witnessed firsthand church rules and protocols being relaxed or altogether ignored to accommodate sheep who had gone astray.

"That reminds me. Did you ever use those checks I gave you just in case there were last minute wedding expenses?"

"No. I didn't need to."

"Okay. Well, I have some more digging to do. Your secret is safe with me. I'll let you tell your father in your own time and in your own way. I'll talk to you later."

"Bye Mom . . . or shall I say Nana."

"That has a better ring to it than Granny. Bye Penny, I've got work to do," said Zoe as she ended the call. Becoming a grandmother wasn't as bothersome as finding out why this money was missing from their personal bank account. She needed to talk to Ben.

* * *

"Hello Velma. I need to speak with Ben. Is he there?"

"No ma'am. He won't be in until this afternoon. He said something about taking care of business. Is there a message?"

"Just have him call me when he gets in. It's urgent that I speak with him," Zoe didn't want to divulge the specific reason for her sense of urgency.

Later at dinner, Zoe waited for Ben to finish eating. She didn't want to pounce on him right away about the missing money, especially if there was a simple and logical reason for the discrepancy.

"Ben, I got a call from the bank today about a rather large withdrawal from our primary house account today. Do you know anything about it?"

"Oh, yes . . . about that. He didn't want me to tell you, but I loaned Gerry the money. He's taken on a lot of overhead with his vision clinics and needed a short-term loan to help keep him afloat. Please don't tell him I told you. He was embarrassed to even ask me for the loan. He's so prideful. Yes, I withdrew the money."

"Okay, well you know we need to communicate things like this if our system is going to work. I can't balance our checkbook if you don't let me know when you're drawing off the account. It doesn't matter what you spent the money nor whom you gave it to. I don't mind helping out family whenever or however possible. But in the future, when you make a large withdrawal, please, please, please give me a heads up. I was this close to initiating a fraud investigation with the bank," she spread her forefinger and thumb slightly apart to convey how quickly she could have made a knee jerk reaction to the launch an official inquiry into the matter.

"I apologize Zoe," he massaged her shoulders after returning his empty plate and silverware to the sink.

"Mmmm. That feels so good."

"It won't happen again. I promise."

"Thank you, Honey," thanking him all the while knowing she would call the bank to ensure it wouldn't happen again. Tomorrow morning, she would march into Black Crow Savings and Loan and implement a $1000 withdrawal limit, because apparently $5000 was a bit too high. If she was to be an effective vanguard of their money and financial health, then Ben couldn't be tapping into their stash secretly. Gone were the days of Edith Bunker type housewives used to being a silent partner managing the household with a weekly allowance. Zoe was going to insist on an equal say so in their finances. Zoe refused to be bullied or relegated to the background by the menfolk. Their monetary arrangement with her controlling the purse strings worked thus far primarily because Ben was a big spender while she was the prudent saver. They balanced each other out.

Chapter 22

Good News, Bad News

"Good morning, I hope you slept well," said Dr. Stone.

"I rested more than usual. It's hard for me to truly wind down in here," said Teddy.

"That's understandable. I have some good and bad news for you. The good news is that you will be ready for release in about a week. Your insurance has only approved another 24 hours of intense therapy."

"Wait a minute! I've been court-ordered to be in this joint AND I get the privilege to pay for it?" Teddy could feel his ire building.

"Not exactly. You'll never receive a bill from us. We're funded by the County. However, if a client has billable insurance, then a claim is filed for payment. What insurance doesn't pay is secured from our mental health grant," Dr. Stone explained.

"So, twenty-four hours. You mean I've only got one more day to be in here?" Teddy was wide-eyed with excitement to regain his freedom. The bar fight that had landed him in jail and subsequently in Phoenix Rising's Intensive Rehabilitation program was just one of the latest displays of his volatile temper. All the pressure from work and home led to a veritable tick, tick boom. Teddy exploded. Because he was drunk at the time, he still couldn't recall why he had pummeled another regular at Papa Jack's. It must've been terribly offensive because the police accounts detailed a seemingly brutal one-sided attack.

"No. It's just not that simple. That's where the bad news comes in. The majority of those therapy hours will have to take place in our regular group sessions. We scheduled you for five three-hour sessions in group, two 2-hour blended group sessions, and five one-hour individual sessions with myself. Do you think you'll be able to take advantage of the group counseling sessions now?"

"Yes. After our first talk, I realize I need serious help. The fact that some here at Phoenix Rising may need more or less assistance getting over this addiction hump should not be my focus. The point is we all are in this recovery program together."

"Good, good Teddy. I see I have been able to get through to you. I need you to realize that when you're on the outside, that's when the real work begins. You'll have opportunity and access to your drug of choice. You'll need to constantly reach within to use the tools we hope to equip you with to resist your urges lest you fall back into the addictive behaviors that landed you here in the first place."

"I'm more than ready to try."

"Prior to your discharge, we have an exit strategy meeting we set up with your immediate family. We'll have to train him or her to be an asset and not a detriment to your recovery. They aren't expected to watch you like a hawk. It's akin to the peer sponsors from Alcoholics Anonymous. When times get particularly difficult, your point person can encourage you and if needed redirect your behaviors if they aren't in line with achieving recovery. Will that support person be your mother?"

"It should be. But I can tell you right now, don't waste your time. She's not going to come here to help me. Until all of this happened, she had no clue I was popping pills. Now that she does, she's made it abundantly clear that she is disappointed in me. She's very judgmental. Kinda like I was with the people in my first unsuccessful therapy group. At least I know who I get that trait from."

"Well, that's unfortunate. Can you think of anybody else you can assign the task of being on your support team?"

"My Aunt Joyce might help. We are a small family. Lately, I only see her during the holidays. Years ago, when I was ten years old, her son and my cousin Bobby died really young in a car crash.

It was devastating for all of us. Bobby was my best friend. She stopped coming around soon after he passed because she said I reminded her of him. But I know if I asked, she would be there for me."

"Great. Do you have a good telephone number for her? We need to schedule your exit strategy session as soon as possible if you're going to be leaving in a week." Teddy gave Dr. Stone Joyce's contact information before they continued with their private session.

"Have you given serious thought to picking up where you left off when your stay here is done? For starters, who will be your doctor?"

"I haven't thought about it seriously. I know I need to be mad at myself, but my doctor and my boss both had a hand in helping me ruin my life."

"Do you find your work rewarding enough to return to where your boss is potentially addicted as well? What exactly do you do for a living?"

"I'm not living out my dream. I am well aware that I am wasting my time and talent in my present position. In college, I met a guy who was a comic book enthusiast and gaming fanatic like me. We tinkered around in our spare time and created a prototype of virtual reality goggles. I wasn't as committed to seeing the whole project through as much as I was into chasing chicks."

"A missed opportunity," Dr. Stone stated matter-of-factly and jotted down notes on his long yellow legal pad.

"Now, I am just an overpaid paper pusher for the federal government. You've heard of the saying 'cutting through the bureaucratic red tape'? My department is in charge of supplying said red tape. We administer federal pass-through contracts. I see your eyes glazing over. Trust me. It's a glorified clerical job, but it pays exceptionally well. I would have an uphill battle finding another position paying as much in the private sector.

There aren't any private entities I can easily apply my experience to. I feel essentially stuck. If only I had stayed on that VR project, I'd be rich now rolling in dough. But I digress. I guess I could request an internal transfer. I just don't wanna start all over again."

"One of the tenets of AA or NA is avoiding the people, places, and things that helped them to become, remain or relapse into addiction. I know changing your job, your primary source of income, is easier said than done. However, if you can be under the supervision of another person, I strongly urge you to take that path."

"I will."

"You don't sound very convincing. The bottom line is you only need to convince yourself. Take my advice. Recognize that if you feel stuck, you have to be the impetus to get yourself unstuck. You'd be surprised how much control *you* have over *your* life. No one is forcing you to live where you live, work where you work, or love whom you love. These are all personal choices. How do you envision taking back the reigns of your life?"

"I just really want to get back to work. After being in here, staring at the four walls most of the time has me missing my cookie cutter cubicle. The work wasn't fulfilling, but at least I was productive there. I was finally on track to move up when all of this happened."

"Is there a special lady in your life?"

"No, I'm just kind of playing the field. Nothing serious for me."

"Honestly, trying to be involved in a romantic relationship is discouraged throughout your first year of recovery."

Teddy's eyes widened. "Really? Why Doc?"

"The initial euphoria of a fresh new relationship can captivate and distract you from tackling the critical issues you need to painstakingly address. As you pack tools into your wellness recovery toolbox, you need to rid yourself of excess baggage and travel light on this leg of your journey. You will be more emotionally fragile and vulnerable. Naturally, you'll be tempted to fill the void with other things that make you feel good. The caveat against relationships is also rooted in the reality that love connections do not always work out well. Unfortunately, if your relationship winds up being unhealthy, challenged or worst-case scenario ends in a break up, then it becomes a stressor that may lead to relapse," Doctor Stone explained.

"That makes sense. A couple of years ago, a woman I fell for really hard broke my heart. I took her to the Polynesian restaurant Kahiki to propose. The setting was classy and romantic. I don't know if I told you Doc, but I love birds. They had live finches flying around in there. The ambiance of the island music and birds chirping was amazing. It was the closest thing to leaving Ohio for a two-hour venture in a secluded tropical paradise. Well, long story short, she turned me down. You wanna know why?"

"Why?" The doctor leaned towards Teddy intrigued by this information. "Yes, please continue."

"She said her parents wouldn't accept me because I was a registered Democrat. Can you believe that? Missing out on a lasting and loving relationship with me because of a political party affiliation. That was probably just what she told me to get rid of me."

"Maybe she couldn't be forthright about refusing your marriage proposal. She no doubt loved you as a boyfriend, but didn't deign to align herself permanently to an addicted husband," said Dr. Stone.

"She didn't even know about the pills."

"Are you sure about that? Addicts tend to operate within two extremes. They're either paranoid that everyone knows about their problem or they absolutely lack self-awareness."

Teddy looked puzzled.

"Do you honestly think your intended wasn't cognizant of your habit? Granted, she may not have known the specifics, but having dealt with families of addicts for years, they know. They know that something is awry. They know when their loved one isn't operating at one hundred percent."

"You're saying she knew I had a monkey on my back?"

"I personally don't like the monkey analogy. Monkeys are small and can be tamed. Some people even find them quite cute. I think of addiction as trying to domesticate a dragon. While everyone else has a typical cat or dog, the addict chooses instead to live with an oddity of a pet. In America, the land of the free and the brave, choices are always honored. Even though it is not rational, others will accept your prerogative to decide how to live your life. If you are willing to house, care for, maintain, and find companionship or comfort in your exotic pet, then more power to you. The lack of self-awareness tells you that walking, feeding and stroking a dragon is normal socially acceptable behavior, when it truthfully isn't. At the end of the day, it is a dragon, a mythical and presumably untameable creature. It's abnormal and judging by the look on your face you realize the absurdity."

"I guess I see your point."

"What happened with this young lady? The love of your life?"

"I left her there in the restaurant. It's a good thing it all went down there. I had wanted to ask her to marry me a month earlier when we went to Vail, Colorado. That's why I dug her so much. I know I am different, but she really vibed with me. Like me, she loved the outdoors. We had a blast hitting the perfect powder there. I honestly felt like we connected on every level. Obviously, I was wrong. I couldn't return the engagement ring, so I had to sell it at a loss. I was beyond hurt. My mother was no help. She said 'No better for you. I told you that you were rushing in too fast.' That wasn't what I needed to hear. I was crushed. I was devastated and went through a terrible bout of depression. I refuse to be simped like that again."

"Simped?"

"Made a fool of like a simpleton. You're preaching to the choir about pressing pause on the dating thing. I can take time to focus on just getting my own act together."

"Oh okay. Teddy, I want the best for you. This one-month program is not an optimal treatment period. Have you heard of the concept called muscle memory?"

Teddy shrugged his shoulders, "I think so."

"When you learn how to ride a bike, muscle memory allows you to replicate that activity even if it's been years since you've ridden a bike. If you ever find yourself seeking out a less than scrupulous doctor who's handing out pills like it's candy, then you'll be riding that bike right down the path to similar bad consequences. This opportunity for diversion, to avoid winding up in a jail cell, is intended to be a wakeup call. In the event your behavior doesn't change this go round, you can and should seek help again. Again and again until you finally succeed. It took you longer than 30 days to get to this level of addiction, so it's highly probable that your road to recovery will take much longer."

"We've been here a while now," said Doctor Stone checking the time on his Bulova wristwatch. I'll work on getting in touch with your aunt. You will need to sign a waiver allowing me to discuss your care plan with her. We'll meet again tomorrow after your group session. Okay?"

"Sounds good," replied Teddy. It all sounded good now. Was it lip service? Like the doctor said, the real work on breaking his habit would only truly be tested once he wasn't in this controlled environment.

Chapter 23

Greed Creeps In

CJ was glad Ben had ponied up the money he requested. He couldn't help but wonder if he could get more. Not from Ben, but from Zoe. He had observed her at their daughter's wedding. Judging by the attendees, Ben and Zoe belonged to social circles of a certain pedigree. From what he knew about the higher-up muckety-mucks, their image was paramount. Zoe had a reputation to uphold. Just the mention of exposing Ben's involvement with him was certainly worth another $5,000 if not more.

He was having his morning cup of joe reading the *Columbus Dispatch* Metro section where Zoe was featured in an article about her community service endeavors. She sounded like she was on a gold star trajectory for sainthood. She had volunteered over a thousand hours at Children's Hospital NICU as a Cuddler. "Rocking the babies is therapy for me, the baby and their parents. Human touch can work healing miracles. I get to talk, sing, soothe and rock a sickly and fussy newborn closer to the day he or she can leave the hospital setting. Their parents who are absent due to time or travel restrictions or other obligations like their other older children can be assured their baby isn't alone while they are away. I sometimes cry when my volunteer shift ends," Zoe was quoted by the local reporter.

As a teacher, literacy was also important to her. Zoe donated her time to tutor adult learners wanting to become competent readers. She and Ben had donated generously to the Columbus Public Library, the Columbus Literacy Council and the Reading is Fundamental Campaign. In what spare time she had left, she fostered puppies that would be trained as guide dogs for the blind. For all of her philanthropic deeds, in a week she was being awarded the Zonta Club's Outstanding Woman of the Year

Award.

Everything seemed to be coming up roses for Mrs. Zoe Eagleston. Was she truly outstanding? CJ pondered how she would react knowing her husband was a sneaky snake in the grass. Did Little Miss Perfect realize that while she sharing her goodness with the world, her not-so-devoted husband was sharing his goodies with another? Swapping her out clandestinely for a man.

CJ decided he would fork out the $100 ticket price to be in the company of Mrs. Zoe Eagleston Volunteer Extraordinaire. He had been a lowly servant when he crashed Penelope's wedding. This time he would invite himself and be served as a legitimate guest.

* * *

"Now ladies and gentlemen, the woman of the hour," said the emcee dressed in a shimmery evening gown. She had given a lengthy introduction of the illustrious what-would-we-do-without-her Zoe Eagleston. The obligatory applause followed as Zoe made her way to the podium to give her acceptance speech.

CJ was growing impatient. Zoe was not the best at public speaking. Her delivery was monotone and her content flat out a boring rehash of her community contributions to date. His rented tuxedo was uncomfortable. Perhaps his discomfort came from trying to fit in with those seated as his table. Or maybe a small part of him was not in congruence with the evil he intended to unleash on the Eaglestons. He was beginning to question why he hadn't taken a more surreptitious route rather than this conniving yet brazen one. In either case, he had gone too far down this path to turn back now.

Finally, Zoe's droning on and gushing about herself stopped and the crowd clapped in earnest no doubt thankful her protracted and formulaic acceptance speech was finally over. CJ sprang into action. He called Ben's after-hours answering service with the code message he used to summon Ben to their rendezvous point. From the concierge station, he waited and watched for Ben to leave the banquet hall. CJ relished in his seducing power to so easily pull Ben away from the leading lady. As a subversive understudy, now it was time for him to pounce on Zoe.

"Mrs. Eagleston I am amazed at all you've done. I'm a patient of your husband's. He's an excellent physician. Well, of course you already know that. They say behind every great man, there's a great woman," CJ offered.

"I like to think of myself as being beside him, not behind him Darling. And you are?" Zoe hated to correct one of Ben's patients who saw her as an ancillary part of their marriage, but she wasn't one to bide her tongue.

"I'm Paul Stevens. I'm a relationship expert. Maybe you and Dr. Ben could give me an interview someday. I'd like to know more about how well you two have navigated married life for what has it been . . . 28 years?" he asked glancing at Zoe's printed bio in the event program.

"Twenty-nine Dear.   Together for thirty-two and married twenty-nine," she said firmly not wanting to be short changed for time served.

"That many?   That's amazing.   I heard you say you like racquetball.   Maybe we could play a few sets while I do an informal preliminary interview. It could just be casual between the two of us. I find women are more talkative and can give baseline details of your relationship.   Then afterwards, I can interview you and Doctor Ben together as a couple."

"Okay.   I'm at the Racquetball club faithfully twice a week. Tuesdays around 5 and Fridays around 1. Will either of those work for you?"

"I will meet you there Tuesday."

"Sounds lovely. I don't know if I have a lot to share about matters of the heart. I'm no spring chicken, but make no mistake thinking I won't give you a run for your money out on the court," Zoe boasted.

"Trust me, with almost thirty years under your belt, I'm confident you'll have plenty to say about married life . . . the good, the bad and the ugly. I promise I won't go easy on you. I might have some moves to keep you on your toes and give you a serious run for your money," CJ chuckled. "I'll see you Tuesday," he told Zoe and then left to meet a waiting Ben at their usual rendezvous point . . . the North High Street Sun Bubble Room Eight.

Chapter 24

Free At Last?

"I'm trusting you to stick to the plan now that you're out. I'll come by and check on you. If I didn't have to look after your Uncle Robert, then I could keep a more watchful eye on you. I wish I had room for you to come stay with us. You know I've never changed anything in Little Bobby's room. It's a shrine of sorts. I just go in there and sit on his bottom bunk. It quiets my mind because in a way he's still with me. Enough about me. You're sure you'll be alright at home?" Joyce asked with concern in her tone.

"I'll be just fine. Mom will be there to support me," Teddy tried to reassure his aunt. He was apprehensive about being released into Joyce's care knowing he would in reality be going home. He knew his brusk mother might not be a great support but rather a hindrance to his full recovery.

"Support? My sister? Support you?" Joyce scoffed. Then her look became serious. "You really believe that don't you?" She had pulled into her sister's driveway behind Teddy's dormant vehicle. It had collected a thick layer of dust while it sat idle. Joyce had retrieved it from the police impound lot the day after he was arrested. So far, she was doing all the positive reinforcing and after care her sister should have been doing. Joyce always thought Thelma dealt with Teddy harshly as a sinister twisted form of punishment for being a carbon copy of his father. She thought it, but never tried to correct or to advise her sister on her parenting style.

"Yes. I do. She's mad now, but she'll come around," Teddy sounded hopeful. He understood his aunt's point. Thelma rarely showed him any tenderness. It was demands, commands, and reprimands. They seemed bound by some invisible contract that Teddy desperately wanted to renegotiate with more favorable terms.

"She never told you . . . about *her problem*?"

"What problem? What are saying? Is my Mom sick? Is she dying? Tell me the truth."

"Oh, my goodness, no! You do take after her. Such a flair for the dramatic."

"What then? What are you talking about? We promised my counselor no secrets back there remember?"

"I know. This is coming from a place of love and I think you need to know . . . that well . . . your mother once had a drug problem. That's why she left her job a long time ago when you were younger."

"What?!"

"She wasn't fired outright because she wasn't the only nurse with access to the Class A drugs. Apparently, she was micro-dosing patients on her unit in order to siphon off enough to feed her own addiction.

"My hope is that you can beat this thing. Just like your mother already has," Joyce said trying to sound convincing. Was she trying to convince Teddy or herself? She wasn't sure Thelma had truly conquered her addiction. It could have been Thelma was just in a state of forced recovery now that she no longer had access to the drugs that were once so readily available to her at the hospital. Maybe she was still using unbeknownst to Joyce. After all, they rarely spoke to or visited one another. Could Thelma hide an ongoing drug habit from Teddy? Perhaps the shame of losing everything had been adequate motivation for her to quit cold turkey. In either case, Joyce hoped this wasn't going to be a case of the blind leading the blind.

"I made a promise to myself that I am going to do my best. I'm the only one who can get in my way. I'm coming back stronger and better," he said. He leaned over and kissed Joyce on the cheek. "Don't worry about me. I'll be okay. You'll see."

"Wow. You took that well. You never cease to amaze me Teddy."

Teddy shrugged his shoulders. "That's a heavy secret to be carrying around, but it does begin to explain a lot. I'm sure I'll sort it out later. Thanks again for everything. I'll give you a call later," he waved goodbye as she backed out of the driveway and headed home.

"Well, well. I guess Joyce was too busy to come in and see about me," Thelma complained as she leaned over to peer out the window.

"Hello to you too Mom," Teddy put down his 'Patient Belongings' bag and softly kissed Thelma on her forehead.

"Don't come in here trying to sweet talk me. I got things for you to do. That crazy neighbor lady kept pestering me while you were gone. She went to the market for me. But I couldn't ask her to go out of her way to get *my* cigarettes. I've been getting by on these generic cigarettes. Why spend good money on smokes you don't even like?"

"Maybe you should have tried quitting altogether. Not just giving up *your* brand."

"Whatever Son. Go get my purse. You can go fetch me some cigarettes and Argo starch," she said still spying out the window like a goldfish trapped in a bowl.

"I'm glad you asked."

"Asked what?"

"About me Mom! About why I nearly lost everything . . . my freedom, my job, my mind. . . over some pills. Doesn't what happens to me concern you anymore? I'm grown, but I still need you. When I've messed up like this, I could use a little consoling. A comforting word. You're acting like I went away on a luxury vacation solely to inconvenience you. I was away at rehab. I desperately need to make changes. Can't you at least acknowledge that?"

"I'm sorry. Do you want an 'Attaboy' for getting clean? I think it's a no brainer that you shouldn't have been doing drugs in the first place."

"Is that what someone told you when you were trying to get clean?"

"Wha . . . wha . . . what do you mean? Me get clean?"

"Come off it Mom. Aunt Joyce told me why you really lost your nursing job."

"She had no right to tell you that. She couldn't wait to make this look like it was all my fault. She's pure evil."

"Quite the contrary. She's been there for me when you haven't. You couldn't even greet me properly when I came in just now. Besides, did you think I would never find out? What I don't understand is why you can't cut me some slack. I'm trying to turn my life around for the better. Nobody is perfect. Not you. Not me. Just gimme a break. Give me some credit for trying to better myself instead of criticizing me all the time. Can you just do that?!" Teddy yelled and gathered his bags from the Phoenix and stomped all the way up the attic stairs. Alone in his room, he could begin to process where to go from here.

Chapter 25

Poisonous Passion

CJ realized he could accomplish his goal without being this up close and personal, but he gained a certain level of satisfaction watching his prey squirm.

Zoe was already warming up on the court. He had misjudged her physical fitness. At the wedding and the awards ceremony, she was clad in flowy evening gowns. Today, she had on a colorfully printed silver and magenta sports bra with matching form-fitting biker shorts that accentuated her curvy yet muscular physique. Apparently, her biweekly sessions at Columbus Racquetball had repaid her handsome dividends in the form of a toned body. For an older woman, she had no cellulite nor varicose veins. Good genes and good fortune had blessed Zoe with a gorgeous body.

"Good afternoon, Love. I had to fight rush hour traffic to get here," he explained as he fished his racquet out of his Coach duffle bag. He was hoping to make a fashion statement. It was a small gesture trying to convince Zoe that he belonged in her monied and elite world.

"No problem, Paul. I thought you might chicken out on the stiff competition," she made a deft move that let him know she was a beast on the court who took no prisoners. "Then I remembered you also wanted a baseline interview with me. So glad you made it," she lobbed another ball punctuating her eagerness to have an opponent to challenge.

"I would not miss this match for the world," he said. He did a few jumping jacks and leg stretches. Clueless about the whole game, sport or activity, he hoped Zoe was impressed by the show he was giving.

"Ready?" She asked simultaneously engaging her racquet with

the ball.

He missed the serve. "No fair! You didn't warn me," he protested.

"If you stay ready, then you don't have to get ready," she retorted.

CJ was out of his element on the court where Zoe effortlessly thrived. He needed to regain the upper hand. He crouched like a baseball catcher at homeplate. His racquet was clutched with a tight grip ready to return whatever Zoe fired at him.

Whoosh. Whack. Whop. Whop. Whop. At least he was able to last a bit longer that time. He needed to catch his breath. "So how exactly did you and your husband meet?"

"We met at Ohio State. I was studying for my degree in Education and he was Pre-med." Zoe served again. Again, he missed.

"College sweethearts. That's cute. You told me where you met, but how did you first meet? At a frat party? A game? In a class? I find a lot of my clients meet by accident and feel the manner in which they met was kismet. Was that the case with you and Dr. B.?

"Everyone thinks Ohio State is a party palooza. We could've met at a party, be we didn't. Back in the 60s, when Ben and I were there, we were both truly dedicated to our studies. However, our meeting was very accidental. My hangout was in the stacks on the top floor in the History section of the Main Library. The smell of the dusty leather-bound books was comforting to me. It reminded me of my grandfather's study. There was a power outage in the building where the medical library was housed. Ben was forced to move over to my neck of the woods at the Main Library. Besides studying for midterm exams, he had a term paper due for his Natural History class. That's when he discovered me in my natural habitat of sorts. We hit it off immediately and have been inseparable ever since. Maybe my grandfather's spirit was indirectly responsible for our love connection," Zoe said.

"At the awards banquet, you said you were together three years before you finally married. Was the delay due to your need to finish college before tying the knot?"

"I guess you could say that. Honestly, Ben would have remained engaged if he wasn't one to keep up with the Joneses. When his brother Gerry married, it really got under his skin that Gerry, his baby brother, was brave enough to do what Ben hadn't. He's always had something to prove as a big brother. It always had to be bigger and better than whatever Gerry did or had. The sibling rivalry didn't start with our wedding, but it has always been obvious.   I imagine if people can have an inferiority complex, then Ben suffers from the opposite, a superiority complex."

"Ah, I see. As his wife, does his competitive nature ever get in the way of your relationship? Is he ever in competition with you?"

"No. Never. We complement one another. I believe it is because we're professionals. I let him be a doctor and he allows me to teach. We both serve people but in drastically different ways."

"Makes sense. So how was child rearing? Did you always agree on parenting styles?"

"We both wanted the best for our three children. Foremost, that meant the best education money could buy. My sons attended St. Charles Preparatory Academy while Penelope went to Columbus School for Girls. I am a teacher at CSG, so I'm sure having me as her mother on campus was an undoubtedly unique experience for her."

"I see," he took mental notes of her marital and parental history. This wasn't an authentic investigation. He wanted to push forward to the real reason he was seeking out Zoe in the first place. Money. He needed to pivot the conversation in that direction.

Whoosh. Whack. Whop. Whop. Whop. Zoe had resumed their match. "Can we finish our game? I'm in the zone," she said touching two fingers at the base of her neck checking her pulse.

"If we keep playing, this is a great cardio workout."

"Okay." CJ was grateful there were no witnesses to how mercilessly Zoe was annihilating him on the racquetball court. He tried to keep up with her, but she was a pro. His mock interview would have to wait. Once Zoe was through beating the dogsnot out of him, they began retreating to the showers.

They reconvened at the juice bar. Zoe had ordered a jumbo smoothie. CJ really wanted a stiff drink but settled for a spinach, carrot, and pineapple blend that was refreshing after their exhausting bout.

"Now that the children are grown and gone, how do you and Dr. B. manage as empty nesters?" he asked. CJ wanted to pat himself on the back for a stellar acting performance. He, of course, knew nothing about relationships. At least not formally. But he'd watched enough Oprah to be able to formulate the poignant relationship questions.

"It may come as a surprise, but I feel like we've rediscovered our passion. Sure, we got bogged down in what it takes to raise happy children into healthy adults. Shuffling them to and from school, practice, and sporting events. If it wasn't the boys playing football, soccer, or baseball, then it was Penelope going to piano, ballet, or gymnastics. We kept them busy. Ben and I always carved out time for ourselves as a couple. I think some call it Date Night. We just called it quality time together."

CJ, playing the role of Paul Stevens to Zoe, was beginning to tire of her fantastic tale of the idyllic family life she thought she shared with Ben. Now was the perfect time to burst her wonderful bubble.

"Speaking of time, how does your husband spend his down time? What is he doing when he's not being a doctor, loving husband and devoted father?"

"Well, I think he could probably answer that question better for you when you interview us both Mr. Stevens," she offered curtly.

Had he struck a nerve? Until now, she hadn't addressed him formally and she had been more than forthcoming with her answers. Knowing she couldn't account for Ben's every waking moment, perhaps she had doubts about what he might be up to in her absence. After all, even if she didn't know the details of his infidelity, CJ was positive her female intuition gave her some inkling that she was not married to a man without flaws. Certainly, the perfect man did not exist. Consequently, Zoe's account of the perfect marriage to the perfect man had to be false.

"Does he golf or travel a lot?"

"Yes, he plays golf every Wednesday when his practice is closed weather permitting," she said.

"What about his Monday lunches?"

"How do you know about those?"

"I'm the one he's meeting when he tells you he's gone on an extended lunch," CJ said matter-of-factly with a smirk of satisfaction. He could tell by her pained look that she was beginning to process the gravity of his intimate knowledge of her husband.

"What? What are you saying Paul?" now she was addressing him by his first name. There was an unspoken 'say it's not so' in her plea.

"I'm saying I'm your husband's secret lover. I've been sharing him with you for a little over six years now. He's not who you think he is," he said flatly.

"Is this some type of sick joke?"

"It's not a joke at all. If you don't want to become the punchline of your hoity toity friends' jokes, I'm offering my secrecy . . . at a great cost."

"What are you saying?" she asked again for clarification.

"I think $5000 a month is a fair price to allow you to continue to live out your contrived fairy tale. Don't you think that is a fair price for a fairy tale?"

Zoe was stunned and silent. Tears began to fall.

"Aw, now don't cry. That is not what I want for either of us. I'm fulfilling some void for Benny you obviously can't or won't for some reason," he said being exceptionally cruel.

"You're lying. He hates being called Benny," she blurted out somewhat loudly. She looked around hoping no one heard her arguing with him. She especially hoped no one overheard her husband's outside love interest taunting her for money in exchange for his silence.

"If I'm lying, then why do I know about the strawberry birthmark at the base of his spine?"

Zoe covered her mouth to avoid letting out a gasp. Indeed, there was only one way Paul could know about such an intimate detail. He was telling the truth about his romantic connection to her husband.

"Now that I have your attention. Let's continue. I expect your first payment in cash in two weeks. I'll meet you in the parking lot of Schooler Park on the far side by the swings. Should you refuse to pay, these pictures will be leaked to the press," he spread out an array of photos of Ben and himself in several compromising positions. The depiction of each erasing any doubt she had about her deceitful husband living double as a closeted gay man.

More tears fell as a previously confident Zoe, sat motionless and helpless to Paul's demand.

He was growing impatient with her emotionally charged response. He slammed his fist down on the pictures, "Do you understand?" he practically yelled in the otherwise quiet juice bar. Fortunately, his ire had not drawn any attention to them.

Zoe nodded.

"You'll be at the park on the first?"

She nodded.

"Now let's go."

Zoe didn't want to go with Paul. She was also afraid not to obey his precise instruction.

It was still light outside when they exited the club. He walked Zoe directly to her car. "How did I know this was your car?"

"I don't know," she shrugged still shell-shocked by the information he had just shared about Ben.

"I have a similar model. It's *your* car. It's your old car to be exact. The leased vehicle you returned to the dealership three years ago. Ben arranged for direct transfer to me. I got it for a song. Thanks for the excellent upkeep by the way. It runs like a dream. I look forward to driving this one too," he tapped on the hood of her car and sauntered over to his gently used version of her current car.

He hopped in his foreign model sedan and revved the engine. "I'll see you in two weeks," he yelled out of the opened window as he rode away from Zoe who was affixed to the spot he had walked her to moments earlier. Where would she go from here?

Chapter 26

Teddy and Thelma Fight

Teddy didn't anticipate that his return home would be such a bumpy transition. He underestimated his mother's intolerance for his imperfection. Knowing she was no stranger to drug addiction made him question his heretofore cozy living arrangement. Could he do it? Was this arrangement ideal? Was it even doable? He decided to go downstairs. Maybe eating a hearty breakfast would help him think more clearly.

He opened the fridge. What he seen was yet another confirmation that Thelma was not going to make things easy for him. She had taken the time to move the contents to one side. She had taped two pieces of paper to the back reading "MINE" and "YOURS". It was clear. She didn't even want to share a meal with him. All that was left on his side were a few bottles of water and a few slices of Swiss cheese. How petty could she be?

"What am I supposed to eat?" he asked as Thelma sat with her back purposely toward him knowing the vast emptiness he'd just discovered.

"I don't know? You should be used to eating bread and water. Aren't those standard prison rations?"

"I wasn't in prison. I was in rehab."

"Court-ordered rehab. It might as well have been prison, jail, lockup. If you weren't free to leave, then it's just semantics."

He sighed. He filled the kettle to boil water. There was a half full box of Raisin Bran he could kill until he got an opportunity to stock up on groceries for himself. He never imagined this setup with his own mother. After all, this was his progenitor, not some random detached roommate. He often wished he had gone away to school. As it stood, he had commuted to Ohio State and never lived away from home. If only he could turn back time and find the appropriate time to make his exit. But here he was an overgrown man fixing a borrowed from boyhood bowl of cereal to eat.

"While you were on vacation," she gestured with air quotes, "a rather irate gentleman came to pay you a visit. Seems like he believes you've been playing the sly fox in the hen house with his baby chicken. Angela was the name he said I believe. What have you been up to with a teen mom named Angela? You preying on pretty young things now? That's sick. Absolutely sick and twisted. I know I raised you better than that."

"How did YOU raise me better? I recall your version of romantic advice being nothing but brief. And I quote, 'Son I don't want to hear about it. Just wash it and keep it clean.' Do you remember that brief speech?"

Thelma bit her lip and had to stifle her laughter. After all, in this moment they were fighting. She put her head down and pretended to ignore him.

"Really? Vacation? You can call it exactly what it was. Court-ordered rehab. It was hard work. It was no vacation at all. Angela is a friend and nothing more. You always jump to bad conclusions when it comes to me. What did you tell the man anyway?"

"I just told you what I said. I told him you were away on vacation and as far as I knew, you were alone," Thelma responded flatly.

"Good. I was definitely away from here, but trust me I was not alone."

"I'm pretty sure he didn't believe me. He left in a huff and all I heard was a blue streak of Spanish. I don't know what he said, but I didn't need to buy a vow or a clue to know his feelings towards you. ¡Adíos mío! ¡Basura! He must have said that three times before he crossed himself and then spat on the ground to emphasize his hot distain for you. He spotted your

Teddymobile in the driveway. When he did, he doubled back towards the porch insisting to talk to you. That's when I had to get Old Faithful out of the corner. Funny how a woman wielding a weapon can suddenly be revered and heard. He turned so fast away from me, this house, and that bat. I got a little kick watching him scurry away. If he catches you in the streets unarmed, then I can almost guarantee you it won't be pretty."

"Well, I'm not worried, because me and Angela are just friends. Nothing more. Nothing less. Believe me," Teddy said trying to feign bravado and convince his doubtful mother that he wasn't a perverted predator. Now he had two angry and presumably dangerous men to watch out for. Ranessa's "manager", Derrick the bully and now Angela's dad. Women he only had a fleeting moment of desire to engage with had placed him plumb in the cross hairs of their disturbed daddies.

At least he knew what Derrick looked like if he was foolish enough to come after him in retaliation for their bar brawl. Angela's father, however, could sneak attack him because Teddy had no idea what the man looked like. Being irate is not an accurate physical description. The same man also had the distinct advantage of knowing Teddy's home address. Nobody wants to be challenged on their own home front. While Teddy wasn't exactly the king of the castle, he was instantly vexed by the fact that his mother had to defend herself. How dare this dude come up on his mother's property like that. What could have happened if she didn't have her handy slugger Old Faithful? What if he had been packing heat? The life-threatening scenarios were stressing him out. He went to the hall closet, grabbed his jacket, and reached in the front pocket. Pay dirt! He found a tiny white envelope from Dr. B's apothecary. He shook it. No rattle. It was empty. He felt defeated and relieved. Defeated that using again was his automatic response to stress. Relieved that he didn't have access to the devil dots or chemical candy to destroy his hard fought for sobriety. Luckily, he had dodged a bullet, but he would have to do better.

"So, you really haven't changed?" Thelma had managed to catch him in the act of trying but failing to pop some nonexistent pills. He was so enthralled in his caper that he didn't even hear her walk up behind him.

"Look. It's empty. You happy? I think you like seeing me fail. It's one more reason to keep me under your thumb. I can't take you and your crap anymore. I'm out this piece!" He flung the front door open and just as quickly slammed it in Thelma's face. In a matter of seconds, he was peeling out of their driveway in his Teddymobile.

"He'll be back," Thelma whispered. She felt a sharp pang of guilt thinking perhaps this time she had pushed him too far. Hopefully, he was headed to Joyce's.

"Joyce. This is Thelma. I need to talk to you and not this machine. It's about Teddy." Immediately Joyce answered. Her answering machine was her method to screen out unwanted calls.

"What's wrong with Teddy?"

"Well, he sped away from here like a bat outta hell."

"Why did he do that Thelma? Tell the truth and shame the devil. What did you say this time?"

"Why do you automatically assume he left because of something I said?"

"Because it's always something you said or did. He called and told me about your icy welcome home last night. You've got to try to be a little more understanding. Tell me what really happened?"

"Well, I told him about this girl's father who came by while he was gone. Apparently, the girl is underage, working on baby number two and had run away from home. He'd seen Teddy giving her a ride home and I guess just assumed they were messing around."

"And you did too? That's why he's mad?"

"Let me finish. He got all in his mangina feelings because I asked if he was into little girls. I told him I raised him better than that and he snapped. I even caught him trying to take more pills," Thelma relayed to Joyce.

"What?! Why didn't you stop him?!"

"There weren't any pills left in the package for him to take. But if there were, I'm positive he would have taken them."

"Listen at you. Positive about your own child's weakness or failure. Do you think he went to see the girl and get things straightened out with her father?"

"No. I thought since you're his aftercare point person or whatever you call it, he'd be headed your way. I just thought I would fill you in because I am pretty sure I will be painted as the villain in his version of events."

"If he comes by here, then I'll let you know. If he does, then maybe he should just stay here for awhile. It sounds like there's too much animosity between you two right now. I've got to get back to Robert. He's not having a good day. I'll talk to you later," as she quietly hung up the phone so as to not wake her husband. When he was able to sleep through the pain, she was hypervigilant to keep the noise to a minimum so he could enjoy whatever amount of peaceful sleep he could get. Rarely did he sleep more than four hours at a time.

She shook her head. Tragically, an auto accident took her son away from her. Granted, Thelma didn't have a rosy life, but she still had Teddy and it seemed like she did everything in her power to constantly push him away.

Chapter 27

Goodbye to Old Rubbish

Paul's demands were a devastating blow. Zoe felt physically and emotionally spent. Less than an hour ago, she was spilling her guts to whom she thought was a relationship expert. Now she felt like a plumb fool. She gladly told a mere stranger some of the basic inner workings of her marriage. He told her the exact opposite. He was Ben's long-term lover. Whatever solid dealings she once thought she had with Ben were now shaky at best.

She didn't know what to do next. What if Ben had exposed her to AIDS? She hoped he had taken precautions to protect himself and then consequently her. The very idea of having to even take a test to confirm she was sexually healthy was daunting. All these years, she thought she was solely involved with only one partner. Now, Ben's cavorting with Paul meant she had essentially been sleeping with any and all parties, male or female, who had been intimate with this shady spouse-stealing scoundrel.

Zoe wanted to scream. She was angry with Ben, herself and that sleazy slimy Paul who thought he could barge into their lives and upset their happy home.

She turned on her car radio. It was playing Sunny 95 FM which was the station she tuned in for the traffic reports as she traveled crosstown from Bexley bound CSG to the Upper Arlington anchored racquetball court. Ironically, Tina Turner's *What's Love Got To With It*? was playing:

Oh-oh-oh, what's love got to do, got to do with it?

What's love, but a second-hand emotion?

What's love got to do, got to do with it?

Who needs a heart, when a heart can be broken?

Zoe had a sinking gut feeling that even gorgeous leggy Tina Turner recognized that the physical acts of love could be separate and distinct from true matters of the heart. Zoe didn't even think her heart could be broken, but here Ben was toying with it all along. She felt less like a confident teacher but more like a colossal fool. What did love have to with this mess? Did Ben really love her? Ever? She mashed the auto channel select button and the radio scanned over to 98 FM The People's Choice.

Now the edgy Eurhythmics were confidently belting out their Number One hit *Sweet Dreams*:

Sweet dreams are made of this.

Who am I to disagree?

I travelled the world and the seven seas.

Everybody's looking for something.

What was Ben looking for in a partner other than her? He often joked that among his colleagues' spousal choices, she was his gorgeous trophy wife. Why was he with a man? Would she feel any less hurt and disgusted if he had betrayed her with a woman instead of a man?

For years, Zoe had been careful to monitor Ben with his office staff. After all, he spent more time with them in close quarters than he did at home with her. She made it a point to drop by his office unexpectedly every so often just to ensure Ben was being a good boy. She genuinely trusted Ben to be true blue to her. It was other possible lady lurkers who might be swayed by his charm, drawn to his good looks, impressed by his superior intellect, and lured in by his wealth and status that kept Zoe on high alert. Had she thought of herself as an eagle-eyed detective when she really had been a long-necked ostrich with her head buried in the sand? Apparently, her monitoring was too myopic. She had suspected nothing. Were there signs her almost three-decade long marriage was crumbling that she had ignored?

Still wanting a distraction, she payed closer attention to the song lyrics. The words were confirmation of her total misunderstanding of a man she'd had loved wholeheartedly.

Some of them want to use you.

Some of them want to get used by you.

Some of them want to abuse you.

Some of them want to be abused.

That refrain wasn't very uplifting or encouraging. Zoe's logical mind knew Ben was her ultimate betrayer, but her anger in that moment was reserved for herself and the slimy slivering person calling himself Paul Stevens. Zoe should have vetted his credentials. After the news and demand he relayed to her in such a cold and calculated manner, she knew he was no relationship expert. He was nothing more than a tramp and a whore. Disparaging labels that had no assigned gender, but fit him well.

She would take back her power. She would not let this scar her psyche as it had her heart. The song's outro mantra was:

Hold your head up

Keep your head up

Movin' on

Hold your head up

Movin' on

Keep your head up

Movin' on

She was not going down without a fight. There was too much at stake. Ben's sexuality and infidelity would jeopardize more than their marriage. Her contract with Columbus School for Girls had a stringent morality clause. Even though Ben was the unfaithful spouse, a public scandal of a well-known pillar in the community could be grounds for termination from her job. The prestigious school had a reputation to uphold. Any staff or faculty member embroiled in legal, moral, or ethical issues highlighted by the media was in grave danger of being asked or forced to leave. She had seen teachers asked to part ways with the institution for far less. Ben's philandering ways could earn her a cold hard case of the blues and a hot-off-the-press pink slip.

"Ben what have you done to me?! What have you done to us?!" After a few minutes of uncontrollable crying, Zoe put the car in gear and headed home. She had to take care of some business. Although she planned to seek out the optimal solution to this conundrum, she wasn't sure it would pass muster as legal, moral or ethical. "God help me through this. Please!"

Chapter 28

Ready To Go Down?

Climbing stairs was not Thelma's strong suit. That's why Teddy could typically rest assured she wouldn't venture from her first-floor window pane perch downstairs to snoop through his room upstairs. Those fourteen narrow steps leading to his bedroom were like a protective moat blocking free entry to his wing of the castle. It might as well have been a rickety rope bridge rigged with explosives . . . highly dangerous and practically impassable to Thelma.

"This boy of mine," Thelma muttered to herself having finally caught her breath. Teddy had a small collection of framed pictures from an assortment of proms and homecomings he had attended as an escort to his so-called friends. "Look at that 'fro," she chuckled to herself. She didn't care for the popular ethnic hairstyle. Thelma felt low cut hair on Teddy gave him a neat and more professional appearance. It was bad enough Black men and boys were the most hated and feared on the planet. If he had a gentler and kinder look, rather than a radical and edgy one, then maybe society would treat him as such. Like the gentle and kind soul she knew him to be.

"Why am I so hard on you?" she asked a 5" x 7" portrait of Teddy in a powder blue tuxedo posing with the girl he had taken to the Brookhaven prom. The girl was lovely, but Thelma despised her. Truth be told, Thelma didn't care for any of the females Teddy dealt with at all. The last one to break his heart was Freda Fivehead Griffin. Thelma would tease Teddy saying Freda must have a lot on her mind. Thinking or not, he jumped the gun and proposed to her way too soon.

A pang of guilt hit her just then. Instead of being comforting, she had only derided Teddy for opening himself up like that. She couldn't be sure if her objection was to his being vulnerable to love or to the possibility of heartbreak or rejection. No matter how hard she tried to prevent it, she knew that someday, somehow, somewhere her baby boy would indeed get his heart broken. Maybe that's why she was so hard on him. Her own divorce was sudden and had crushed her. Deep down, she never wanted Teddy to be in a position, albeit a typical rite of passage, to fall in and out of love, to hurt like that. Her intentions were well-meaning, but it all just drove him away.

She started opening dresser drawers to see if he had any hidden stashes of pills. Joyce had asked her to do this before Teddy came back from rehab. She had agreed, but had no intention of checking his room for contraband. She wasn't confident that if she found anything that she could resist the urge to experiment with her pharmaceutical findings. Even though she had been away from that life, she knew her inner addict was only comatose and not dead. It could be revived at any time with the right inducement.

Thelma decided to peep into his computer. Taking a seat at his desk was a wild ride. No sooner did her bottom hit the padded seat, than she plunged down about six inches. "Whoa!" She wasn't ready to go down . . . not like that. Her heart was racing. She pushed keyboard buttons until she heard it waking back to life. Her cybersleuth mission was thwarted quickly. The blinking cursor in the password box of the sign-in page locked her out before her electronic intrusion could even begin.

She opened his wardrobe and found a picture of herself. Upon closer examination, it had tiny pin pricks in it. Teddy had been using it as a makeshift dartboard. "The nerve!" She slammed the door shut. She wasn't sure what a room inspection would yield at this point. She had lived with him and never knew he was hooked on pills. Whenever they disagreed before, he had never stayed away long. Being in his room, gave her a semblance of connection. She missed him and she didn't want to miss him anymore. Being in his "hands off" area was the makeshift reunion she needed to ease her mind that his absence was temporary. His stay at the Phoenix had brought on a crippling loneliness for her. If it had not been for Ouida, she's doubted she would have survived.

"If he finds me up here . . .," Thelma said to herself making sure everything looked as it was when she got there. She clicked off Teddy's desk lamp and hit the switch for the light above the staircase. She turned sideways and started going downstairs one step at a time. If Teddy pulled into the driveway right now, she'd be caught in the act moving at this pace.

Thelma was holding onto the railing trying to balance years of extra pounds on the tiny narrow steps. The wood groaned under the added pressure. Because it was Thelma and not Teddy, the stairs were a makeshift alarm creaking to announce her foreign footsteps. The attic light flickered and then went out altogether. "Oh shoot!" Thelma was now halfway to safety. If only she could focus in the dark and reach the final landing. She gripped the banister with her right hand and planted her left foot down. Or at least she thought she did. In a panic, she released the banister trying feebly to break her inevitable fall.   There was tumbling, crashing and finally a thud. To Thelma, everything had faded to black.

Chapter 29

Everybody Is Looking For Something

"I'm here to meet with Councilman Mulholland. He should be in the private dining area I believe," Henry Butler told the host at the check-in stand of the Marble Gang restaurant. The eatery had become a posh gathering spot in the Mount Vernon Plaza. It was a gemstone anchor of the strip mall. After featuring John X in the outdoor atrium selling oils and incense, the indoor complex was home base to a medical clinic, a post office, a barber shop and a bank. It was modern retail and office space dedicated to serving the community. The Marble Gang just so happened to be serving soul food staples at a premium.

"Yes, he's already here Sir. Follow me, please." Butler followed him to an awaiting Skip Mulholland. He always could appreciate someone who valued his time. Too often Black folks fell back on honoring CP Time and it irked him.

"Hey Man. Good to see you. How you livin'?" Butler greeted Mulholland with a hearty handshake.

"I'm doing well. Join me," he nodded at the empty seat across from him at the table. "I was glad to see you at the community meeting. Turnout was fabulous. I expected you might chime in as a landlord and resident, but there were plenty of people there with plenty to say even if you didn't."

"That's true. But I've got the inside connection," he winked at Mulholland as he placed his maroon linen napkin on his lap. "I know my old college buddy is going to take care of me and mine," Butler's diamond pinky ring glistened in the ambient light.

"Well, that's what I wanted to talk to you about. The current plans will spare your residence. Your property is too close to the water table of Alum Creek, so it is safe. But as for your properties further down Nelson Road, that's a different story."

"How different Man? I'm paying you swell to stay ahead of this thing and look after me in this deal. After all, we can't just let the railroad and grocery store be the only ones walking away as fat cats off of this deal," Butler said taking a sip of the Manhattan he'd ordered.

"Yes. So, here's what is going to happen. The apartment complex on the east side of Nelson will be leveled to make room for the project. You'll be compensated handsomely for it . . . at least two to three times its estimated fair market value to account for lost future earnings."

"Keep talking."

"The government, state and federal, I'm not quite sure which yet, will also pay you to assist your current tenants with their relocation efforts."

"Why me? Why not pay them directly? I don't want the headache."

"It's just easier to write one check to you and then you in turn disperse the funds as you see fit."

Butler's weasel eyes lit up. "Really?" He quickly popped a bite of steak into his mouth. He washed it down with a bit of water before finishing off his Manhattan.

"So, they could pay me say a thousand dollars per unit for relocation assistance and I disperse, oh say half of that and the rest I'll call administrative costs?'

"Not exactly, but yes, something like that."

"You said the complex to the east, but what about the one on the west side of Nelson?'

"Obviously, there will now be additional noise associated with the 670 Project. Even people who are used to living next to noisy trains will find it a major adjustment to have a busy thoroughfare practically in their backyard. The truth is you may lose tenants on that side of Nelson too. In the event you have problems maintaining occupancy in that complex, you'll be eligible for compensation under an urban revitalization program. Essentially, you'll lose control of one property, but get paid. On the other hand, you keep the other property with the same result – you'll get paid."

"Sounds like a win-win situation. What's the catch?"

"You need to make some capital improvement and do upgrades on both properties. The tenants who eventually will be displaced need to believe their apartment homes are not in the path of the looming freeway construction. Eventually, there will be no place to stay per se, but you don't want them to fly the coop too soon. If they all start leaving, then your property value will plummet and diminish the compensation you will be entitled to be paid. Upgrades to the parcel on the west side of Nelson will benefit you in several ways. You'll be able to justify raising your rental rates, increase the property value and that increase will boost the amount of losses you will ultimately be compensated for as the landlord."

"What kind of improvements? I need to know we're on the same page. Are we talking about a new roof, plumbing overhaul, or minor cosmetic improvements?" he asked and snapped his fingers to garner the attention of their server. He needed another Manhattan. "I'll have another please. More whiskey this time. My first one was pretty weak. I wanna taste my liquor otherwise I'm just drinking juice. Last I checked this was a bar and grill and not a juice bar," he said gruffly.

"Yes Sir. Right away," the server hurried off with the empty glasses.

"I'm sorry. You were saying," Butler refocused his attention on Mulholland who was wolfing down his perfectly seasoned oxtail soup as if it would be confiscated in retaliation for Butler's curt and rude treatment.

"I'd say you should go with what could be removed, reused or resold. Things like windows, screens, locks or carpet."

"Gotcha."

"This of course has to stay between us," Mulholland leaned over and whispered over the flickering dinner candle.

"Of course," Butler replied waving a newly cut piece of steak on his fork. "Same price as usual?"

"Well, the usual is fine, but I was thinking about tossing my hat in the ring to run for mayor. How would you like to be the first to grease the wheel by oh say . . . doubling your usual campaign contribution? One in your name and one in your wife's to get around the donation cap."

"Damn Man! That's a lot of bread!' Butler slammed his fist on the table.

Mulholland was startled and jumped as if threatened. He hoped no one heard Butler's outburst.

"I got you though. You've been looking out for me, so I'll look out for you. Truth is my grandmother always told me I was cut out to be a pimp or a preacher. I honestly like this hustle better," Butler said.

"Wow, she had that much faith in you?" Hammond asked. They both laughed. Having discussed the true business at hand, the two relaxed into the unrehearsed rhythm of random conversation. They reminisced on their college days. They got into the usual 'Who Shot John?' stories that got covered in the *Call and Post* but never the *Columbus Dispatch*. The two didn't realize how much time had passed until the bartender announced, "Last call for alcohol!" from the front bar.

Chapter 30

Departures and Arrivals

"Thomas, I think we should let Ben and Gerry know what's going on . . . sooner rather than later," Elena said gently as she held a icy cup of water for him to quench his thirst. He refused to reveal their financial instability to his incredibly wealthy and successful sons. Worrying about his security had taken a toll on his health. The aging lovebirds were now keeping each other company at the Harrisburg General Hospital.

Thomas had suffered a mild heart attack after learning his pension fund was in danger of being folded along with the remaining assets of Lebanon Steel. The Pennsylvania company was yet another casualty of Trickle-Down Economics. Due to the onslaught of cheap foreign-produced steel and the decline in the country's demand for it, steel mills around the country were being closed down and boarded up in record numbers.

The once steady stream of income had skipped the trickle stage and flowed to a complete stop. Thomas' sons would not comprehend how the recession had affected their parents.

"I don't want them seeing me as a burden. This too shall pass," he managed to say perched upright in the repositionable hospital bed. Elena was fluffing his pillow to make him somewhat comfortable.

"Please don't say 'pass'. Not here. Not now," she pleaded as tears welled up in her eyes and fell down her wrinkled face. Her eyes weary from being at Thomas' side. Although he was a prideful man who never complained, she felt his angst. She knew how unfair it was to invest over thirty years of time, sweat and energy into something trusting, hoping and believing for a great payoff that never happened. For Thomas, that payoff was to be his retirement. He used to talk about plans for his golden years all the time. Plans to travel, to fish, and to tinker with his father's old boat and motorcycle. All plans she knew were indefinitely postponed because the gold for his dreamed of retirement was tarnished and could possibly vanish altogether. She was the silent witness to his defeat and subsequent physical demise.

"Where's the doctor? I can't stay in here. They'll charge me nine dollars for one aspirin," Thomas said angrily as he tried to swing his covers off and stand up to get out of bed. As he did so, several beeps were emitted from the medical gadgetry he was involuntarily tethered to.

"Thomas, you must rest. Please get back in the bed. You're not well," she implored him.

A nurse came to reinforce Elena's directive. "Mr. Eagleston, where exactly do you think you are going?" asked his nurse, Yolanda, poised with her hand on her hip annoyed at his defiance of the doctor's orders to remain in bed.

Thomas bristled. He resented being scolded like a child by either woman. He felt powerless. "I guess nowhere. You caught me."

"Good thing I did, because you're not dressed for the weather at all," said the nurse tugging on one side of his opened hospital gown.

Thomas blushed profusely. Both women laughed. Their laughter was infectious and he laughed too despite his embarrassment over his foiled attempt to make an escape.

* * *

"Look Daddy. She's got your thick black hair, but hers is curlier," Penelope pointed out to Ben.

"Yes, I guess she does," he said running his fingers through his own hair. Ben went to the sink, rolled up his sleeves and washed his hands and arms up to his elbows as if scrubbing in for surgery. "May I?" he asked reaching out to hold his newborn granddaughter.

"Sure. We've named her Bethany Elena," she beamed offering the baby girl to him.

"Ah, my Wren. You're gorgeous," he said softly.

"Wren? That's different. Why Wren?" Penelope sounded puzzled.

"She's a breath of fresh air. A rebirth. Believe me this little lady has been here before," he said as his newborn bundle of joy wrapped her tiny fingers around his pinky. Her eyes were closed, but her gentle touch confirmed their bond.

"I am a witness, she was just born a few hours ago," Penelope chuckled.

"Tsk. Tsk. Don't worry Wren. Your mommy doesn't realize you time traveled here to save us. We'll teach you about this world and you'll unlock the secrets of the universe for us. Thank you for coming," he whispered softly to his firstborn grandchild.

"Wow, Dad. You're banking on a seven-pound infant doing quite a lot."

"Just wait. You'll see Penny. I thought my life was full as a husband, a father of two boys, and a physician. I thought I had it all. The day you were born changed my whole thought process. Having a daughter taught and gave me two things.

I now had a different female, other than my mother and wife, who could command my heart in a profound way. While I loved and cherished your brothers, they never had me wrapped around their little finger like you, my Love."

"I get it Daddy."

"Ahem. Do you think I might be able to get in on this Love Fest? She's my granddaughter too," Zoe interrupted.

"After you wash your hands ma'am, you may," Ben demanded

sternly.

Zoe sighed but relented and followed the doctor's orders. She cradled little Bethany. She tucked her receiving blanket snuggly. Her volunteer post as a cuddler had taught her that newborns love to be swaddled. She touched Baby Bethany's forehead and tiny fingers and whispered to her, "Just perfection."

Chapter 31

A Big Fat Check

"D o you renounce Satan?" inquired Metropolitan Parelli of Baby Bethany who was wide-eyed and shivering as he held her precariously in the baptismal basin.

"I indeed renounce Satan, " responded Todd, Penelope's older brother, Bethany's uncle. He was speaking by proxy for the infant child as her godfather. Naturally, the baby lacked the ability to even comprehend such forces as good and evil. This was her ceremonial entry into the Greek Orthodox faith. It marked the day she became a Christian even though it would be years before she could absorb the gravity of this sacred ritual.

After the christening, there was a small reception in the church fellowship hall. Small meaning it didn't include decorations or a DJ like a wedding reception might, but otherwise it had all the same bells and whistles. It was a fully catered event with a select group of family and friends.

"Excuse me Mrs. Eagleston. Metropolitan would like a word with you," said Growlin. He had on his Sunday best. He typically invited himself to special occasions of the other parishioners. No one seemed to mind. Most pitied him and his wife, Cora. It was his job to clean up after such affairs, he figured he might as well benefit.

"Mrs. Eagleston, congratulations on your new family addition. I pray you were happy with the service," he said soliciting her approval.

"Thank you Metropolitan. I was very pleased. I want to present you with this check. It's a donation for the Church's Building Fund," Zoey said handing him a personal check for $15,000.

"Wow!" he said all but snatching the paper bank note from her dainty hands. Too bad it was Sunday or he might make a beeline to the bank with it. "I mean thank you. This is a lot more than we agreed upon earlier."

"Well, five is for your services and ten is for the building fund. I trust you will be discreet," Zoe said with a raised eyebrow to convey her concern.

"Definitely. These things happen all the time." 'These things' meaning babies created prior to holy matrimony. "The Father understands. He appreciates atonement," he said. He couldn't wait to exchange this tiny token piece of paper for valuable Treasury notes. He could almost smell the cash. His discretion might lead to a different distribution than the one Zoe suggested. More like ten for him and five for the church. The Reclamation sanctuary, narthex and atrium were riddled with paintings, silver-plated plaques and gilded replicas of religious relics with "Donated by" or "In Memory of" engraved placards on them. If given the chance, Metropolitan would acquire said items wholesale and then pocket the rest. He had become quite adept at convincing families who were in a particularly giving mood to let him handle the fine details of their contributions. As long as he produced something tangible in exchange for their giving, be it sincere or disingenuous, then it was not donated in vain.

The scandalous payoffs for absolutions by church leadership were a common practice dating back to the Dark Ages. Though shameful, it was an unspoken custom for ministers of faith to promise to absolve sin in exchange for the almighty dollar. To the other members of Reclamation Church, it would appear as if the Eaglestons had made a heartfelt sentimental charitable donation to the parish. Only Zoe, Ben and Metropolitan would be privy to the ultra shady and not so pious behind the scenes deal.

Chapter 32

Feds Swoop In

The lobby was overflowing with anxious patients waiting their turn with the good doctor. Even those who absolutely dreaded doctors would consistently show up for their "examination". It wasn't the desire for physical health that drew them there, but they needed their fix in a dispensary bottle to keep them going.

The door chime atop the front entrance kept sounding in rapid succession. Six agents clad in navy blue DEA vests had arrived. They were on a serious mission and each one was holstered.

"Ma'am, I need you to step away from your station."

Velma hung up the phone mid conversation and complied.

"Where is Doctor Benjamin Eagleston?" he read from a document. "I have a warrant for his arrest," he asked in a calm baritone voice.

"He's in Room Four with a patient," she pointed to direct the dark-haired man who was clearly in charge of the takedown operation. She wanted to warn Dr. B., but it was too late.

The agent proceeded to Room Four. He opened the pocket door without knocking or announcing himself. "Doctor Benjamin Eagleston, you are under arrest."

Ben gulped. All color drained from his face. "Wh- what is this all about?" he asked as he was turned around and handcuffed. His patient was partially clad. Dressed in only a paper gown, she slinked off the exam table, grabbed her coat and purse, and left before the agent could give any more details.

"You're being placed under arrest for Medicare and Medicaid fraud, conspiracy to commit intrastate insurance fraud, and illegal distribution of pharmaceutical drugs," the agent then recited Ben his Miranda rights.

Patients were murmuring as they were led out of the building. "But I am out of my medicine. How can I get a refill?" said one blue-haired older woman.

"It's a doggone shame. I hope nobody sees me here. I don't need to get caught up in someone else's mess," a matronly looking Black woman said as she waddled out to the safety of anonymity in her car.   Ironically, here getaway vehicle was a rusted out Corsica that displayed a black and gold WWJD bumper sticker.

Inside, the office was filled with foreign sounds. Computers were being unplugged and removed. File cabinets were quickly being opened. The metallic boom from rapidly being slammed shut once emptied was startling. One by one, the drawers were rummaged and the contents were being boxed up. The onsite pharmacy was the epicenter of the invasion. Pills rattled as they were tossed into cardboard boxes. These would not be used for their intended purpose. Perhaps they never would have been used for a salient purpose. They were potential evidence now.

The door chime was being overworked. The sounds of scurrying footsteps leaving were announcing that trouble had arrived. Trouble had come so they had to go. After all of the patients had vacated the premises, Dr. B. was escorted out of his medical office building. He felt helpless and embarrassed as he squinted at the sunshine unable to shield his eyes. Eyes. The watchers. He had thought no one was watching. Apparently, they were. How would others see him now? Zoe? His children? Wren, his precious granddaughter? His staff? He began to weep.

"Save the tears for later. They don't move us," said the arresting agent who protected Ben's head while shoving him into the back of his unmarked vehicle.

Chapter 33

The Numbers Don't Lie

His once fledgling medical practice was now working like a rather well-oiled lucrative money-making machine for Dr. Eagleston. There was an influx of patients to his Hilltop medical cottage style facility. They were male and female, Black and White, young and old. What they all had in common were two things. Billable insurance and prescription drug coverage. Line 'em up, get 'em in, and get 'em out. Repeat.

What Eagleston didn't count on was Drug Enforcement Agency oversight. Rules promulgated by the federal agency would become the proverbial cog in his wheel. He had an onsite pharmacy that dispensed the "uppers" or diet pills his steady stream of regular customers were clamoring for. He felt like the in-house pharmacy would help him fly under the radar of the State Pharmacy Board and the DEA. In the early 80s, President Ronald Reagan had declared a War on Drugs. Initially, street drugs like crack and heroin were being targeted as the menaces to society. Later, it became addictive pain medication and finally the abuse of prescription drugs. Until this era, it was almost a foreign concept for people to believe doctor-prescribed medications could be classified as addictive substances. What once seemed like a benign issue had developed into a malignant cancer creating addicts and destroying families.

The public service campaign of "Just Say No!" spearheaded by First Lady Nancy Reagan was not the only countermeasure taken to combat the scourge of drug abuse in America. Big Pharma was being called to task over the onslaught of prescription meds. As such, sophisticated lock out tag out controlled substance dispensers became prevalent in hospital distribution of Class A narcotics like morphine. It acted as a deterrent to medical professionals who might divert the expensive, powerful drugs to themselves or others for purely recreational use. Additionally, there was more scrutiny by the Food and Drug Administration over where these drugs were ending up in the supply chain. That's how the slip shod operation of Dr. Eagleston was finally exposed.

Between 1979 and 1981, he had prescribed and dispensed over 2,000,000 doses of amphetamines, popular pills known to be a highly addictive synthetic inducer of serotonin. That's roughly thirty patients a day receiving a 90-day supply of "speed balls" or "bennies". The fact that one sole practitioner's office was pushing out roughly 20,000 pills of the same drug in a month to its patients was glaring evidence of medical wrongdoing. An above-board doctor, who adhered to his oath 'to do no harm', would undoubtedly be writing scripts for an array of meds be it pain killers, antibiotics, diuretics, blood thinners and supplements. The fact that the stimulants were prescribed did not render them harmless. An evil vicious cycle was created. The doctor's greed grew in direct correlation to the people's need to feed their habit.

It was an oppressively hot August day in Columbus. It had taken years, but the chickens had come home to roost for Dr. Ben Eagleston. Time had slid quietly into 1985 before the good doctor was made to answer for any of his misdeeds. Nothing in his world was normal. Vacations abroad had been cancelled. Zoe remained in the marriage, but she was aloof and emotionally detached. His gigolo was missing in action. His once booming private practice was defunct. Once a confident and accomplished man, he was now reduced to being an insecure and disheveled mess. His only ally, his attorney, was undoubtedly by his side because he was paid handsomely to do so. This hollowed out, colorless version of Dr. Ben wished he could time travel back to the exact moment he himself had set these tragic series of events in motion. Hindsight indeed was 20/20.

"Doctor! Doctor! Do you have any comment on your disciplinary hearing before the State Medical Board today?" asked an eager television news reporter shoving a parabolic microphone towards Ben Eagleston trying to get an exclusive. None of the other media outlets bothered to cover the westside pill mill scandal. The truth was Eagleston couldn't officially be called a doctor anymore. He had voluntarily surrendered his license to practice medicine. He could, however, regain his license and be in good standing if he took two years of continuing education classes and passed a federal medical licensing examination. He was grateful that he was not subjected to a harsher punishment. He had already decided to fold his practice. Being that Eagleston was already sixty years old, he had no immediate plans to attempt to have his professional licensure reinstated. That would be tantamount to starting all over. Passing the State Boards some thirty odd years ago was a harrowing feat. He didn't even want to imagine the mental fortitude required to regain his credentials at the federal level. Ben had decided instead to partner with his younger brother, Gerry, in his franchised optical clinics he had opened around town. It wouldn't be the same as having his own practice, but it was decent, steady, and honest work.

Ben's lawyer was the only one to address the reporter and his accompanying camera man with a resounding, "No comment!"

Chapter 34

Help Me Help You

Gail was anxious to return Dr. B's phone call. She'd been reading about the DEA crackdown on his westside office. When his practice was raided and shut down, she had to scramble to find a new physician.   After her nervous breakdown, she had abandoned his infamous B-12 treatments. Nowadays, she stayed mellow and even keeled with over-the-counter St. John's Wort. She called the number she carefully jotted down from her nearly full answering machine. As usual, she fast-forwarded past the nagging bill collectors and annoying telemarketers. Judging from the exchange, one originating from the far eastside of town, she surmised this was his private home number.

"Hello. May I speak with Ben Eagleston, please?" Gail felt strange not referring to him as Doctor B, but the reality was he in fact was no longer a licensed physician. The *Columbus Dispatch* had made that knowledge public.

Gail could hear shuffling on the other end as someone went to bring Dr. B to the phone. "Hello. This is Da . . . I'm sorry," he stopped himself mid-sentence. "I mean Ben Eagleston speaking. How may I help you?" It would take time to grow accustomed to introduce himself as anything other than a full-fledged doctor. It was as if he was a god or superhero no longer cloaked in immortality. Coming to grips with being a mere mortal would be an arduous process and harrowing task.

"Hello. This is Gail Evans, a former patient. I'm returning your call. You said it was urgent," sounding somewhat perturbed as she wanted to quickly conclude their business.

"I need to speak to you about a fellow you referred to me awhile back. A Theodore Robinson I believe. He's been identified as a key witness for the federal prosecution in my case. You're his supervisor, right?"

"Yes. He is. I am not sure how I can be of any help to you. That's a private matter," Gail said dismissing his plea to involve her in his treacherous legal affairs.

"Hear me out please. I desperately need to speak with him. I understand your desire to distance yourself from this whole mess. But if I go down, then there will be a ripple effect. Not only will I be exposed, but so will you and Teddy. You wouldn't want that would you?"

"Oh. I see your point. What exactly do you want me to do?"

"We need to convince him to either not testify or to downplay the whole situation."

"I am not sure if I can convince him to do that," Gail knew hold strong willed Teddy could be. However, she did manage to keep Teddy's position in their agency. He would have been fired if he held a similar post in the private sector. Feeling partly responsible for his journey into the abyss of prescription drug addiction, she felt like the least she could do was preserve his job. As far as everyone else in the office knew, Teddy was on medical leave. She squelched any rumor mongers who said otherwise.

"We must. Please arrange a meeting. The sooner the better. I need to stop him from testifying. He's educated, employed and an articulate witness. A triple threat."

"I'll see what I can do," Gail sighed heavily into the receiver.

* * *

"Hey Teddy," she greeted him and then took in a healthy swig of her coffee.

"Hey yourself," said Teddy flatly. The waitress took his order. There was an awkward moment of silence between them. "You said you had something for me."

"I know coming back to work can be tedious. I pulled some strings and got you a new security badge, so there's one less hassle to deal with when you get to the building on Monday morning," she handed him a laminated badge on an embroidered Ohio State Buckeye neck chain.

"Nice touch. Gail, but having known you for years, why can't I shake the feeling that you are trying to butter me up for something?"

"Well, I . . .," she barely managed to say looking up as her eyes met the approaching Doctor B as he walked up and joined them at their table by the cozy fireplace in the 256 Highway Cracker Barrel. She hated to lure Teddy like this, but she sincerely felt it was the easiest way to arrange what the good doctor had proposed.

"Mr. Robinson, I told Gail it was imperative that I meet with you. To the State, I've already lost my license and credentials to practice medicine. But now they're trying to prosecute me on the federal level. They want to take away my freedom," Ben's voice cracked.

"As they should. Do you think I care about your fraudulent ass getting locked up? Man, miss me with that. I'm not some junkie with needle marks on my arms, legs, and toes, but sometimes I think I might as well be one. I lost my girl, my freedom temporarily, and almost lost my job behind these pills you were passing out like candy. I'm positive that I nearly lost my mind."

The waitress reappeared with their entrees. The interruption eased the tension momentarily. Gail pushed her fork around in her salad. Teddy didn't eat, but instead only glared at Doctor B.

"I can never say I fully understand your situation, but I heartily apologize for my part in it. I'm simply asking for you to help me . . . strike that . . . help us reign in this whole situation. We could all end up behind bars. Losing everything. You don't want that do you?" He glanced at Gail and Teddy.

"Is this the part where I am so supposed to be eternally grateful for you saving my job?" he turned his gaze towards Gail who had fallen silent since Ben joined them.

"Listen to him Teddy. If they find out that I referred you to him, then I'm sunk. If I go down, then you go down. All of my hard work to pull strings and cover for you goes down the drain. We'll both be out of damn good jobs with excellent pay and benefits."

"What exactly are you two asking me? How can I ignore everything that has happened? And why should I?"

"If approached by the authorities, then downplay everything. I'm not asking you to lie per se," Ben pushed an envelope with cash towards Teddy. "Call it a little forgive and forget. I just think we can come to a mutual understanding of this unfortunate set of events," Ben hoped Teddy could be persuaded by cold hard cash. It had never failed him as a way to get out of messy jams in the past.

"Man, you are so lucky right now that I fully understand that flipping this table is not in my best interest as a Black man dining at Cracker Barrel. That's why you invited me here? Right, Gail? So I wouldn't cause a scene? Well, I can't be bought for a chicken dinner and some biscuits you jive turkey! This isn't worth my life," he said shoving the envelope back at Ben. "My silence nor my soul are for sale!" Teddy left the table and restaurant in a huff.

"Well, that didn't go well," Ben said surprised that Teddy had refused his usually fail safe bribery.

"You don't say," Gail said rolling her eyes at him. "Damage control is not your forte. I hope you have a better solution to get in front of this," she said to Ben. "Waitress, can I get a box for this? I've suddenly lost my appetite."

Chapter 35

On the Run

"Derrick had been stalking Teddy trying desperately to seize the moment he could retaliate for his brutal beatdown at Papa Jack's months earlier. He had followed Teddy to the Pickerington Cracker Barrel. As he entered the gift shop for a much needed restroom break, he bumped into an obviously perturbed Teddy headed directly toward the parking lot. He seemed distracted and focused at the same time. Clearly, too focused on whatever or whomever had him so irritated that he wasn't aware of anyone in his pathway . . . not even a big buff guy like Derrick.

"Hey Man! Watch it!" Derrick exclaimed.

"Watch it yourself!" said an already irate Teddy as he pushed past Derrick and continued toward the exit.

Fed up with being bested and ignored by Teddy, Derrick followed him out of the restaurant. He wasn't fast enough to catch Teddy before he got in his vehicle and left.

Derrick caught up to Teddy at the traffic light. He followed close behind. But as it was dusk and the backroads had no street lights, he proceeded with caution. Unfortunately, Teddy had not done the same. His unchecked speed meant disaster as he approached and became yet another victim of Deadman's Curve.

As Derrick watched Teddy's car leave the roadway, he felt instantly vindicated. His nemesis had finally met his karma. He was candidly aware that given their violent history, he'd be a suspect if any harm came to Teddy. His first instinct was to flee. Run and never look back. Remembering all the kicks and blows he'd taken from Teddy, he couldn't feign concern for the man. He didn't even check to see if Teddy could have been saved from the wreckage. He was a man without a conscience and just kept going.

Ranessa! Ranessa! Where are you?!" Derrick yelled upstairs.

"I'm right here where you left me. What's the matter? Are you ready for Round Two Big Daddy?" she sauntered downstairs to greet him with a long juicy kiss.

"Get off me woman! There's no time for that right now. We've got to get far away from here. They'll be looking for me. For us."

"Who exactly are they? What pray tell did *we* do? Fill me in please on the details."

"Please Ranessa. Just pack your things . . . only the bare necessities and let's go."

"Like these?" she opened her silky robe revealing her cocoa brown naked body.

"Damn you look so good right now," he said biting his fist. "But we need to hit the road and get as far away from this place as possible."

Ranessa, who had a voracious sexual appetite, was not obliging any of his pleas to pack up and go. Instead, she dropped her robe entirely and pushed him down on the bed. He couldn't restrain his carnal urges anymore. He let her do what she did best. She laid her head in his lap. "Girl, you are going to get us both killed. But at least we'll die happy," he whispered as he moaned and ran his hands through her hair. Their escape plan would have to wait.

Chapter 36

Ouida Alerts Authorities

Two police cars arrive at the Bennett residence shortly after Ouida calls them. She is concerned about Teddy. She knows he has returned to the clutches of Thelma after being in rehab for a short stint. She hasn't seen him coming and going as usual. When Ouida took Thelma a dinner plate, she told Ouida he left in a huff. According to Thelma, he claimed he needed to go clear his head. It was mid-morning and his car was still gone. Ouida hoped that wasn't code for him being so frustrated with her that he was forsaking his 40 days of being clean and trying to go get a fix. After doing errands for Thelma for only a short while, she could totally empathize with Teddy. She considered herself a non-drinking and non-smoking straight arrow. In the short time of dealing with the impossible-to-please perched paragon, she could see why Teddy used whatever substance. She could only guess because he had never divulged his bad habits with her. Probably because he viewed Ouida as a mother figure and it wasn't a kosher subject they would likely share as cordial neighbors.

Her concern grew when she didn't see Thelma at her usual hot spot front and center in the bay window of their kitchen. Ouida usually would wait to see Thelma on guard before approaching to check on her in the morning. She didn't want to meddle, but she had a gut feeling that all was not right with the odd mother and son pair next door.

"Good morning Officers," she greeted the law enforcement pair. It was a man and woman duo. She was envious. She grew up in an era when women were never expected to be more than housewives. If they had jobs outside of their homes, they were clerical, domestic, or menial manual labor positions. She herself had to be taught to drive when she was well into her thirties by her second husband. Times had changed and now a modern-day professional woman stood before her. This pretty lady cop had a badge, a gun, and her own patrol car. Oh the places she would go and people she would arrest if she could wield that kind of power. But for now, she was doing the proper neighborly thing. She wanted to make sure everything was okay in the Robinson household.

"We received a call that you are concerned about your neighbors. You haven't seen or heard from them in how long now ma'am?" the male officer asked as he took out his notepad to jot down any pertinent information that Ouida could give them. His badge was 1313. Not a good sign thought Ouida.

"That's just it. I haven't seen Teddy since the day before yesterday. So that's two days ago. I took Thelma dinner last night.   She's sickly and I pop in and check on her. She is a permanent fixture in that window. But she hasn't made her appearance yet today. That's not her routine. If Teddy isn't there that makes me doubly worried about her. She won't answer the phone either. Can you go check on them, please?" she said with worry and concern in her tone.

"Yes ma'am. Are there any pets or burglar alarms we should be aware of on the premises?"

"No," she volunteered. She could not shake the feeling that something was very amiss with her brother's neighbors.

"Okay, we'll go check it out for you," said the lady cop as she smiled in an effort to comfort Ouida that they would be handling the situation.

The officers approached the Robinsons' porch and knocked. There was no answer.   From Ouida's perspective, it looked like the one officer was talking on his police radio awaiting further instruction. With her hand perched on the handle of her holstered revolver, the lady cop was peering in through the window and then yelled to her male counterpart, "Call for a bus now!" Then with one deft move she kicked in Teddy and Thelma's front door. She kicked it so hard it was like she was entering to find her own philandering spouse. You could tell this wasn't the first time she'd pummeled a plank of wood to gain access.

Ouida watched from afar. The ambulance arrived. Several more police cruisers arrived. Cruiser lights were engaged, but no sirens were blaring. The silence was indeed deafening. Then sadly, the City coroner arrived. The worst possible case was unfolding right before her eyes. After Thelma's sheet clad body was rolled out, the police returned to speak with her further.

"Ma'am. We will need more information from you. We found your neighbor, a Black middle-aged female, deceased at the bottom of her attic staircase. It appears she suffered a terrible fall."

"Oh no!" Ouida exclaimed clapping her hand over her mouth. She felt sad and wanted to cry, but she had more questions to ask and of course probably answer.

"Since it was an unattended death, an autopsy will be performed to pinpoint the actual cause and time of death. Do you know her next of kin?"

"That's just it. Her son Teddy, her only child, is her next of kin. I don't know where he is. Neither did she. They had a falling out and he didn't come home the other night. You're gonna have to find him. I pray he isn't dead too. This is all too much," she said collapsing onto an Adirondack chair on the covered porch.

"We understand ma'am," offered the monotone male officer.

The female officer rubbed Ouida on her back. "Ma'am do you need a moment? I realize this isn't exactly what you expected when you called us. Should we go inside? Get you a glass of water or a cup of coffee?"

"No. I will be alright."

"What makes you think the son Teddy may also be dead? Do you suspect foul play?"

"Oh no. It's just that he recently came back from court-ordered rehab in a facility. Thelma didn't talk about it much. He was supposed to get clean. I didn't really see him much when he got home to notice a difference. I never knew what demons he was trying to purge. Occasionally, I would see him all slicked out to go to the bar on the weekend. But I never seen him drunk. If he was ever high in my presence, I never knew it. He never seemed faded out on that pot or reefers the kids smoke. So, I can't tell you what he was recovering from exactly. Poor thing really needed to get out from under Thelma's thumb. But not like this," she succumbed to the gravity of the situation. She started crying uncontrollably.

The Officer Reid, the stoic male officer flipped his notepad closed. He grabbed an arm as did his partner and led Ouida back into the house. Ouida wasn't a spring chicken. She was more like an old hen with very heavy wet feathers. Lifting her was a mini workout. They lowered her slowly into a brown overstuffed recliner.

"Lawd Jesus! I can't believe she's gone. Why didn't I check on her earlier? I can't take it. This is too much to bear. Fix it Jesus!" she implored her Saviour looking upward through her fresh flowing tears.

"Here. It's going to be alright," said Officer Janae. She had gone to fetch Ouida a cool glass of water. Water and Kleenex. She felt it was the least she could do. Her partner was visibly perturbed by her kindness. He viewed her tenderness as a womanly weakness.

"Well, we have to be going. We've got paperwork to complete for the precinct and the coroner," he cleared his throat signaling Officer Janae to play along and make a prompt exit.

Officer Janae rolled her eyes and asked, "Are you home alone?

Perhaps there's someone we can call for you. We don't want to leave you here by yourself in this condition."

"My no count brother will pop by later. He's at his girlfriend's spot chasing that p. . . I mean cat. She's good enough for giving up that monkey, but can't cook worth a damn. He'll come home to eat, but he'll leave right back out again," she explained now bereft of tears.

The two officers were stunned at how quickly she morphed from grieving friend to judgmental sister. Ouida's word choice was amusing.

"As long as you feel you'll be fine by yourself," Officer Janae managed as she suppressed her laughter. She didn't think she had ever heard the words 'cat' and 'monkey' referenced that way.

"Chile, I'm over sixty. I've lost my share of husbands, family and friends. One more ain't gonna crush me. Sure, it hurts, but in time it'll be alright. We all gotta go that way sometime."

"Here's my card. Just call if you need anything," she said showing off perfectly manicured acrylic nails. Clearly, Officer Janae was clinging to and bringing every ounce of femininity she could to this male-dominated masculine post.

"Thank you Darling," she said rising to see the pair out and bolt the door. She was totally enamored with Officer Janae. If only she could turn back time and join the police force.

Chapter 37

Gotta Save Some Money

Zoe was headed to Schooler Park to meet Paul for their monthly rendezvous. This ordeal was becoming expensive. She had to do something about it. She didn't want to be exposed but she also couldn't justify throwing thousands of dollars out the window to protect their fragile public image. That money would be better spent buying savings bonds for Bethany's college education.

"I've got a little something for you," Zoe pulled out a fresh prescription pad. It was one of the remnants from Ben's office. "Those pills you take . . . they've got a particular street value, right? Why not cash in on that?"

CJ's eyebrow raised. He had never given any consideration to becoming a pill peddler. Upon hearing Zoe mention it, he was instantly intrigued. "How?" he asked anxious to accumulate even more than he intended to collect from her.

"You fill these tiny tickets out for a thirty, sixty, or ninety day supply. The more volume, the greater the savings. The drug stores try to make it seem like they're doing you a favor. If they see you twelve times a year or only four, they'll still be paid. Paid handsomely I might add. Anyway, I digress. You fill the script, then sell the meds for double or triple your costs. Profit, profit, profit. On top of that, with this you can walk up to the pharmacy counter and get whatever you want: uppers, downers, ludes, muscle relaxers, pain pills or tripsters."

"Tripsters?"

"Pills that will take you or presumably your customers on a high-flying trip . . . no airline ticket needed," Zoe informed him.

"Sounds too good to be true. What's in it for you?"

"Honestly, this arrangement is pinching my pennies into copper dust. I may be married to a doctor, but I'm operating on a teacher's salary. I don't want to tip him off to this little scheme between us. Basically, I propose taking my donation down to say $2000 a month. I'll provide you with a fresh prescription pad. They're watermarked and printed on security paper. Wanna see?" she held out the tiny pad for him to examine.

"No. I trust you," he replied waving the pad away.

She was hoping he would trust her. "These come fifty to a pack. You do the math. The possibilities are endless," Zoe could see he was more than willing to explore this new strategy. One thing she could rely on was his greedy nature. He had already honed in on her man. He wanted and acquired people as well as possessions, but nothing was ever enough. He always desired more. He thought he deserved more. He felt entitled.

"Okay. I'll need the full amount today and we'll *try* this way out," he said all but snatching the miniature tablet of empty prescriptions out of Zoe's perfectly manicured hands.

"Well," she let out an audible gasp. "Okay, but I assure you this is a win-win for both of us."

"Okay," he said returning to his car and zooming off into the setting sun.

Zoe shook her head as she adjusted her rear-view mirror to leave. "Such a fool", she spoke to her own reflection. She wasn't sure if she was playing the fool for trusting and believing Ben or if his manipulative money hungry lover was the fool for trusting and believing her. In either case, time would tell.

* * *

"That double-crossing bitty," he muttered through clenched teeth. CJ couldn't quite grasp how he had been bested by a woman. He used the script pad one time and that one-time use cost him his freedom. He was arrested immediately when he returned to retrieve his filled prescription. Apparently, Zoe had failed to inform him that the same script pad she'd provided to him had been reported as stolen or tampered with to the State Pharmacy Board.

"I'm sorry. Did you say something?" his cell mate Marvin leaned down from the top bunk to see if CJ was indeed speaking to him. The pair had chosen not to be friends, but to coexist amicably. Marvin's first question to CJ was "So are you gay for the stay?" Marvin was disappointed with CJ's flippant response.

"Nope. I'm all the way gay, but you're just not my type," replied CJ with brutal honesty. CJ's instant rejection served to draw a clear line in the prison sand between them.

Chapter 38

Breaking the Bad News

"They found another one at the end of Dead Man's Curve," said Sally Henson, a Licking County tech at the Coroner's Office.

"Wow. You would think by now people would learn to slow down like the signage says. But no, they disregard the signs and flashing lights and end up as roadkill in that same old ravine off 256. How long was this one out there?" asked Darla Eddy, her curious co-worker.

"Just a couple of days. I heard when they went to notify his next-of-kin, that person was deceased as well."

"That's doubly tragic for whomever was next in line to get that death notification," said Darla. She couldn't imagine how sad that part of a deputy's job must be. Being the bearer of bad news like that had to be grueling and unfulfilling.

"That's not the half of it. When they did track down that secondary contact, they wanted absolutely nothing to do with the deceased. . . the first or the second one. Apparently, they had been estranged for years. He told our department in no uncertain terms that he wouldn't be claiming either of the bodies. Can you believe that?"

"Let me guess. Not a close relative?"

"No. It was his son and ex-wife. Go figure."

"That's really messed up. Family trying not to be family and denying one another in death," said Darla shaking her head.

"Good thing they were already dead, because a betrayal like that is definitely a stab in the heart," Sally remarked. She turned up the radio to dispel the negativity in the air. Death brought out the ugliness in people. Fortunately, her music was the soothing calm force that got her through the day.

* * *

"Mrs. Joyce Deveraux?" the uniformed officer inquired. "I'm Officer Pritchard from the State Police."

"Yes. What can I do for you Officer?" she was instantly worried about Teddy. He hadn't been checking in with her as promised. Being busy looking after her husband Robert, she never got around to reaching out to him either. She couldn't help but think she should have never agreed to be his aftercare support person.

"Can I come inside? I have a few questions for you."

"Certainly," she said and motioned for him to be seated on her country style brown and beige sofa. She sat across from him hoping Teddy was alright.

"Well ma'am, the truth is there's been a tragedy. I'm sorry to inform you that both your nephew, Theodore Chauncy," he read from one form, "and sister Thelma Constance," he read from another document, "are no longer with us." He exhaled a long sigh of relief having been able to deliver the heavy message in one coherent sentence. He was reading their names off of long forms aided by cheap drugstore readers.

"What? What happened?!" Joyce asked as she slumped in her chair with disbelief.

"Apparently, your sister was found dead in her home Sunday morning after a neighbor placed a call to the police to conduct a welfare check."

"Let me get this straight. He didn't kill her?" Joyce decided to ask. As badly as Thelma treated Teddy, especially in light of his new found recovery, Joyce wouldn't blame him for finally snapping under his mother's overbearing pressure.

"No. No. Not at all. It seems she died as a result of a horrible fall. No foul play was involved."

"Oh," Joyce sat up a little straighter in her chair. "What happened to my . . .Teddy?" her voice trailed off as she broke down sobbing in tears. The gravity of the news was beginning to register and settle in for her to mentally absorb.

"That part we're not so sure about. We found him deceased in his car in a ravine in Pickerington. Do you know why he might have been in that area?"

"No. I have no clue Officer," she mumbled softly as she dabbed at the corners of her teary eyes.

"Well, I just need you to sign acknowledging you've been informed of their deaths. From there, we can get the ball rolling so you can claim their remains for burial."

"Hold on a minute. I see how I'm next-of-kin for Thelma, but Teddy's father is still alive. Doesn't he have legal say so over him?"

"Unfortunately, when notified he made it abundantly clear that he will not be coming forth to claim either body. As a gentleman, I cannot repeat what his actual verbiage because it was crass and offensive."

"He always was a bastard and a buzzard with more than a dash of ugly. I never got what my sister ever seen in him. I guess it's par for the course. Yet again, he leaves me holding the bag to clean up his mess. Such a loser. Thelma really could pick 'em. Losers that is."

Not wanting to belabor the process or navigate messy family matters, Officer Pritchard redirected Joyce to the paperwork he needed her to complete. She filled in the pertinent information and affixed her signature to the triplicate form. It looked like a doctor's signature or passable chicken scratch. He tore off and handed her the bottom copies of each, gave his condolences and then left as quickly as he came. Joyce shut the door behind him. Now she had two funerals to plan.

Chapter 39

Give Me A Memory I Can Use

"**G**ood morning Miss Elena. I'm glad to see you. Looks like you rested well. You ready to get started on your way?" asked Sharon. She knew the feeble minded and bodied Eagleston matriarch was not going anywhere, but asking always got her pumped to get into their morning routine.

"I guess so," said Elena weakly. It was a physical challenge for her to be rolled, changed, washed and dressed.

Sharon had generally taken care of hospice patients. When Dr. Eagleston hired her nine months ago, neither of them thought this would become a long-term assignment. Elena had been gravely ill and insisted Ben take her out of Memorial Hospital to die comfortably at his home. It just so happened that Mrs. Eagleston's earthly time wasn't complete. Maybe it was the top-notch care of her companion care specialist, Sharon, who kept her from coasting so easily into the hereafter. Sharon was relieved to have a steady charge to keep. Admittedly, losing patient after patient took an emotional toll on her. In a way, Sharon was blessed to be working with a geriatric living on borrowed time.

Sharon was especially gentle with Mrs. E. Between her osteoarthritis and brittle bone disease, even a vigorous sponge bath could make her sore. Sharon, or more accurately, the cook would serve Mrs. E. a hearty breakfast while she changed her bed linens. Depending on Mrs. E's stamina, Sharon would wash her up in bed or give her a tub shower. In either case, Mrs. E. would spend the rest of her morning in relative comfort with the help of some pharmaceutical pain relief be it Dilaudid or Valium. She remained in a zombie-like state until lunch. Lunch for a ninety-year-old was bland gruel or tepid soup. No longer could she tolerate the extremes of spice or heat in her diet. When she made it to the Pearly Gates, Elena prayed Saint Peter was waiting with roasted lamb with fresh tzatziki sauce, braised carrots and flaky nut and honey-filled baklava. She hadn't enjoyed any of those Greek delicacies in ages.

"Mum, do you want to sit by the window? It's such a beautiful day. Sharon didn't wait for an answer. She rolled Elena to the nearby window. Her rear-facing bedroom window overlooked an ornamental grapevine and ivy-draped bleached birch trellis that Ben had placed in his meticulously maintained garden. Next to it sat a sculpted water fountain that attracted all kinds of birds: robins, sparrows, goldfinches and grackles. Although it wasn't meant to draw them, squirrels loved the refreshing man-made aquifer too.

Just as Sharon set the brake on her wheelchair, a red cardinal suddenly appeared. Elena's eyes widened and she looked away.

"What's wrong Mum?" Sharon asked a ghostly-looking Elena. She sensed that Elena was frightened by something.

Elena pointed with her crooked wrinkled forefinger towards the crimson bird and muttered, "Red bird means death is coming."

"Mum, that's just a silly superstition. How many of those bloody fowl have you seen in your lifetime? You're still here accounted amongst the living. You'll probably outlive me," Sharon said softly trying to distract Elena's attention from the tiny creature's random landing she had viewed as a foretelling of impending death. Her own grandmother subscribed wholeheartedly to many of the nonsensical notions from their old country, Haiti. She knew not to severely challenge another's firm beliefs.

"Don't worry Mum. I'm not going to let any harm come to you." Elena's narrow shoulders relaxed as if Sharon's words had at least momentarily comforted her and quelled her anxiety.

"I remember when I started working here for you and Dr. Ben. I was nervous to be working for rich, White folks. My own grandmother told me about being an elevator operator at the

Neil House downtown. The White people acted like she was invisible. They only parted their lips to tell her what floor they needed. They never said hello, please or thank you. Can you believe that?" asked Sharon as she paused to gently brush Elena's thin gray hair into a low ponytail.

"Then there were just as many dreadful stories about the people she worked for as a domestic. She told me most days they treated their family dog better than her. She worked her fingers to the bone: cooking, cleaning, laundering and minding children who weren't her own.   Her reward was a measly amount of money, or 'token pay' as she called it, that she could use to buy nylons and enough tokens for crosstown bus fare to do it all over again."

"Listen to me yammering on. I'll get you a lap blanket." She retrieved a cozy fleece throw and draped it over Mrs. E's alabaster wiry and emaciated legs. She knew it could be a bit drafty for Elena near the oversized window.

"You and Dr. Ben were nothing like the monsters she spoke about. You hear me, Mum? You're a joy and Dr. B is so kind and generous.

Elena feebly smiled at Sharon. Her conscious ability to ascribe personal worth based solely on race or skin color had faded with her advanced age and declining health. Now, as she sat at the mercy of her colored caretaker, the stigma of race was irrelevant to either woman in the moment.

"Thank you," Elena said with eyes brimming with tears.

"You don't have to thank me Mrs. E.," Sharon carefully wiped tears away from the corners of her own misty eyes. "I'm just glad I got a chance to meet generous, good, and genuine folks like you and Dr. Ben. Had I not met your family, I would have continued to believe every word my grandmum told me. I like to live fairly. I think we all do. I know Grandmum was absolutely right when she said 'You never know who is going to bring you your last crust of bread to eat or cup of water to drink'."

For what seemed like hours, the two sat in each other's company taking in the tranquility of the tapestry of nature outside. Birdwatching was a shared respite that offered both a glimmer of hope and grace in an otherwise cruel world.

Chapter 40

The Closing of a Lifetime

"Well, just sign here on the dotted line and you'll be the proud new homeowner of 1444 Cliftonfork Avenue," Marcia Hoy said at the closing held at Executive Office Place.

"Oh, I'm so excited. I can't believe this," Ouida flat out lied. She had single-handedly ran off every potential buyer of Thelma's place. It was easy to do.

She'd mosey over to the house when she seen potential buyers approach. "I'm not sure you want to go in there. It's haunted. It didn't end well for the previous owners. I'm trying to move out myself," she would say in a somber tone. Once their interest was piqued, she would make up an elaborate fabrication about Thelma and Teddy both tragically dying in the home on the same day. Each retelling was more devious than the next. She would always end with, "They didn't tell you? They're supposed to tell you. It's the law," she'd tell the potential buyers with a straight face as if her motives and intentions were pure.

It was a ruse that was never earnestly questioned. None of the prospective buyers ever examined. Why would she lie? She lied because she had no home to return to in Louisiana. She'd lie because her brother whose aid she'd come to several months ago had the audacity to live and not die. She truly thought she would inherit his home. But in order to inherit, someone must die. Thanks to her care, her brother Freddie had recovered fully. Fortunately, he was gracious to keep constant company with his ladyfriend, so Ouida essentially had the house to herself. But that wasn't an arrangement guaranteed to last forever. Besides, Ouida wanted her own. After all, she'd done for everybody else, she felt like she deserved it.

How did she swing the down payment? With filthy lucre. She didn't have to wait on the official closing for access to the Robinson's home. When Teddy was away in rehab, Thelma gave Ouida a key. It was to make it easier for Ouida while helping Thelma in his absence.

"What if you fell and then couldn't get up? At least I could come in and be able to check on you if God forbid something like that were to happen to you," Ouida capitalized on Thelma's physical vulnerability. That was her MO or *modus operandi.* If she didn't prey on their physical weaknesses, then she sought out their mental insecurities. Over the years, her bread and butter was filling the void for lonely and desperate people whose greatest fear was one of abandonment. For Ouida, it was a chain of suckers. All the people she fooled fell for her acts of kindness, but they rarely saw she had attached a hefty price to her rendered services.

She had tried without success to reel in both Teddy and Thelma. Teddy was a little too spry and alert to succumb to her usual antics. However, after his death, Ouida was able to cash in on his comic book memorabilia. The proceeds of which were the bulk of the down payment on the home. She was indeed tricky, resourceful and clever.

FOOTNOTE

♥ Malcolm "MJ" Harris. (2022, February 8). *She Was Rude to Marco* . . . #Storytime. [Video] Facebook.

CALL TO ACTION

Thanks for selecting and reading Misplaced Danger: A Fatal Prescription. If you enjoyed the book, please leave a review on Amazon.com. While there, please follow me on my author page for updates on future releases.

Follow me on social media:

Goodreads ~ Marla Morris author page
Blogger ~ Marlaz Memoz
TikTok ~ marlamorris3

BOOKS BY THIS AUTHOR

His Dream, Her Nightmare

Our romantic choices do not always serve us well. This is even truer when duty or tradition rather than authentic love compels one to stay in a toxic relationship or marriage. Winnie is determined to stand by her man Nelson even though he doesn't value her worth as a woman nor her loyalty to him. To honor her vows, she is committed to him despite his criminal past, infidelity and controlling ways. At her tipping point, when she is ready to finally leave their imbalanced union, Nelson won't let her. Winnie disappears suddenly after they celebrate his milestone thirtieth birthday. With the help of his crafty lawyer, Nelson is able to stave off suspicions of her family, friends and most importantly the authorities for years. He is able to live his happily ever after as a free man until he meets his karmic end.

Sweet Burial: The Tragedy That Lies Beneath

Sometimes we bury our deepest emotions, old relationships, and deadly secrets. Married couples in discord often disagree yet manage to discuss their problems amicably. If they cannot resolve the marital conflict then they may opt for divorce. Unfortunately, that is not the logical path Christian Wright chose after entering into wedded bliss with Chloe Abbott. Shortly into their unified journey, they realize they are unequally yoked. While initially there's no physical violence between them, their relationship is rife with emotional, verbal and psychological harm. They seek counseling and are on the verge of ending it all when they learn Chloe is with child. Sadly, the birth of their son isn't the blessed event they hoped it would be. Their child is differently-abled. Chloe embraces their son, while Christian rejects him as if he is a defective toy. A flimsy facade of family perfection is perpetuated to outsiders looking in for years. There is nothing Christ like nor morally correct about the deadly choices Christian Wright ultimately makes forever turning his family's lives upside down.